THE DOCTOR'S CLAIM

A BILLIONAIRE SINGLE DADDY ROMANCE
(BILLIONAIRE'S PASSION BOOK 1)

ALIZEH VALENTINE

HOT AND STEAMY ROMANCE

CONTENTS

Blurb	v
1. Chapter One	1
2. Chapter Two	7
3. Chapter Three	14
4. Chapter Four	21
5. Chapter Five	33
6. Chapter Six	44
7. Chapter Seven	50
8. Chapter Eight	54
9. Chapter Nine	58
10. Chapter Ten	63
11. Chapter Eleven	68
Sign Up to Receive Free Books	74
Preview of Destined Desires	76
Chapter One	78
Chapter Two	83
Chapter Three	90
Other Books By This Author	101
Copyright	103

Made in "The United States" by:

Alizeh Valentine

© Copyright 2020 – Alizeh Valentine

ISBN: 978-1-64808-023-4

ALL RIGHTS RESERVED. No part of this publication may be reproduced or transmitted in any form whatsoever, electronic, or mechanical, including photocopying, recording, or by any informational storage or retrieval system without express written, dated and signed permission from the author

❀ Created with Vellum

BLURB

Alex

Billionaire trauma surgeon... you'd think it would get me some time off to enjoy myself.
Unfortunately, this holiday, I'm heading up to White Pines, Wisconsin to see my family. I end up on the goddamn bus, protecting a cute little thing from an asshole who's getting grabby.
I don't take too kindly to people pawing at what's mine, and from the minute I lay eyes on pretty Chloe Becker, I have a feeling she's meant to be mine. Then I find out she's got a baby in her, and, other man's baby or no, something about a sweetly breeding girl just drives me wild.
She's an innocent girl, whose idea of fun is burgers and star gazing... Maybe before the holiday season is over I can show her what kind of fun I like to get up to.

Chloe

I just wanted to meet up with my sisters and decide what we were going to do with Grandma's house. Things were already going to be tough enough telling my overly-accomplished sisters that I was pregnant and looking forward to single motherhood.

Then there's an asshole on the bus, I'm pretty sure things are going to get nasty, and out of nowhere comes Alex Reed.
He's a billionaire trauma surgeon from one of the richest families in White Pines, so what's he want with me?
As it turns out, he's got plenty of ideas, beginning with his c*ck and ending with me flat on my back.
This is going to be one wild holiday!

CHAPTER ONE

Chloe

The bus was late getting to our stop, and the half-dozen other people waiting with me were restless. Three weeks before Christmas, the freezing Illinois air caused every breath I exhaled to turn into dragon-like steam. I imagined telling my future son or daughter that we were descended from dragons, and the idea made me smile a little as I touched my stomach through my thick coat.

Just two months along now, my baby was a whopping three centimeters long. Despite my circumstances, despite the fact that in about 8 hours I was going to need to spill my whole sorry story to my sisters, I was still giddy. My oldest sister Mara liked to say that I had about as much sense as a Jack in the Box, and maybe she was right, but nothing was going to stop me from being happy about having a little boy or girl as a Christmas surprise.

Anxious as I was about confronting my sisters, I also really wasn't looking forward to the six-hour trip up to White Pines, Wisconsin, but nothing could dampen my spirits—nothing, that is, until I saw the man watching me through the crowd. There was nothing obviously wrong with him. He was dressed nicely enough and wasn't bothering anyone. It was just the way he watched me, not even bothering to hide it.

I'd been using the bus long enough that I could spot a problem, and this man, staring at me like I was a chicken dinner, was definitely going to be a problem. He grinned as if being caught staring was a good thing, and licked his lips. When I scowled, he only laughed, and just as the bus pulled up, he started towards me. The idea of being stuck in a seat with that guy all the way up to White Pines was not my idea of a good time.

I looked around desperately as the bus driver ticked our names off of his clipboard and started loading the bus. There were so many empty seats on the bus, and the creep was practically right behind me. I walked past a college couple and a pair of sisters sharing their seats, then past a mom with a cranky toddler. My eyes swept from seat to seat, searching for an escape. There! Beside a man reading a newspaper, there was an empty spot.

"Hi! Is this seat taken?"

Newspaper Guy looked up in surprise, but before he could answer, I stuck my bag under the seat and sat down.

"Thank you so much!" I chirped, and smiled as the creep skulked off to find another seat.

"It might have been taken," my new seatmate said pointedly. "At the very least, did you miss the dozen other completely empty seats around us?"

A moment ago he'd merely been my escape route. Now I actually noticed that he wasn't much more than twenty-seven or twenty-eight at most, with sandy blond hair and dark brown eyes. He wore a black wool coat that looked expensive, and unlike most of the men on the bus who wore jeans and boots, he wore slacks and dress shoes. I realized he looked like a man who should have had a sleek Mercedes or an Audi or something. So what was he doing on a bus to nowhere, instead of flying first class, at least?

His eyebrows arched irritably—I didn't know eyebrows could be irritable—as he waited for me to answer him.

"Sorry about this," I whispered. "There's a creep who looked like he wanted a seat with me, and I'm going to be on this bus for six hours. I'll get out of your hair later, all right?"

I thought, best case scenario, that my seatmate would go back to his newspaper, grudgingly letting me keep the sanctuary I had found. Instead, his dark gaze sharpened, and his frown deepened.

"What did he do?" he asked, and I blinked at the slight growl in his voice.

"Nothing much," I hastened to add. "It's just he was staring at me, and um... he licked his lips." When I said it like that, it seemed really minor, and for a moment, I thought he was just going to roll his eyes and kick me out of his seat to fend for myself.

Instead he nodded, eyes still narrowed. He straightened enough so he could see over the seat backs, scanning the space like some kind of hunting animal.

"The one in the Packers jacket?"

"There's like four guys getting on in Packers' jackets..."

"Brown hair, glasses, weird little beard thing?"

"Ah, yes. How can you tell?"

"He's staring hard at what he can see of you from where he's sitting. I think that's just your foot and your shoulder."

Self-consciously, I tucked myself a little farther into my seat. It had the effect of bringing me closer to my seatmate, who was still scowling at the creep behind us.

"I'm going to go..." He started to rise, and a fast vision of a bus brawl raced through my mind.

"No, don't worry about it," I said, reaching out and tugging his coat to hold him back. "I just want to make it to White Pines without any problems."

He frowned at me, and then reluctantly nodded.

"Here, take the window seat," he said gruffly, peeling his coat off. "And give me your jacket, I can stow it above."

"Sir, yes sir," I mumbled, but I did as he said. I did feel safer against the window, and I was more comfortable after I had taken my coat off.

"That's simply ridiculous, a grown man harassing a girl your age," he growled, and it was such an old man thing to say, coming from such a young guy, that I laughed.

"How old do you think I am?" I asked. I might not have made the most mature first impression, but I didn't have *that* much of a baby face.

He looked me over, and shrugged.

"First or second year at the University of Illinois?"

I made a face.

"I graduated from college three years ago. I'm twenty-four," I said. "Want to see my license?"

He shot me a very patient look.

"Have you thought that showing strange men proof of address and identity might be a bad idea?" he asked pointedly.

He wasn't wrong, and Mara's weary comment about common sense and Jack in the boxes ran through my head.

"I promise you, I'm twenty-four," I said. "And my name's Chloe. There. Not even a last name in case you turn out to be a stalker or something, alright?"

I startled a surprised laugh out of him, and I immediately liked him a little better. When he smiled, it eased some of the lines around his eyes and made him seem less surly. More inviting. If I was going to be utterly honest, it sent a brief ripple of warmth through me, enough to make me want to blush a little.

Dammit, I thought. *Paul broke up with me three weeks ago, this is way too soon.*

Not for a rebound, a sly little voice replied, but luckily it shut up when he offered me a hand.

"Alex," he said by way of introduction. "And it's a pleasure to meet you, Chloe."

"Pleased to meet you," I said, taking his hand, and that might have been my first mistake. The moment I touched his hand - large with long, slender fingers and a surprising hint of roughness in a man so well-dressed- a spark shot between us. It was like a shooting star, a hot yellow streak through an endless field of blue, shocking enough that I jerked my hand away, wide eyed.

At first, I thought I was just behaving like a freak, but from the startled expression on Alex's face, I could see clearly that he felt it too.

"Static electricity," he said finally. "It's dry in here."

"Yeah," I agreed, but I sensed that neither of us believed it. "Are you going all the way up to White Pines too?"

Wrong question. His face closed like a door, and even in the warmth of the bus, I felt a chill. He might as well have hung a *none of your business* sign on his face.

"Yes, I am," he said curtly, and returned to his newspaper.

Well, at least I didn't end up trapped in a seat with the creep, I thought. I pressed close against the window so that Alex would have plenty of room, and because in my hurry to get to the bus stop, I had forgotten to grab any of the books I was reading, I had to content myself with watching the scenery. Because it was northern Illinois, however, the scenery was mostly scrubby, flat or suburban, so instead I ended up covertly watching Alex, which was much more attractive.

He wore a plain gray sweater that looked so soft that I barely stopped myself from touching it. His shoulders were broad, and I could tell that his hips were narrow. He was lean, but there was some serious muscle on him, if his shoulders and thighs were any indication.

I sneaked another peek at him, and this time I froze because he was looking back at me, his dark eyes dancing with amusement at having caught me staring. This time I could feel a red blush creeping up my cheeks, and I felt about as old as he had thought I was.

Mumbling something about being tired, I turned around completely, curling up towards the window.

He chuckled, and the sweet dark sound sent a shiver up my spine. I closed my eyes. If I pretended to be asleep, he couldn't catch me doing anything else that embarrassing. Soon enough, reality caught up with pretense, and I was drifting off for real.

He's so classically handsome, I thought drowsily, in that random way that happens right before sleep, and then I was gone.

CHAPTER TWO

Alex

When I looked closer, I could tell she wasn't a teenager. She was still younger than I was, but there was a womanly grace to her, in spite of the way she giggled and blushed. Usually that kind of thing annoyed me, but for some reason this time I couldn't help laughing.

She turned her back to me and curled into a tight ball, nothing but a loose blue sweater, jeans, and a puff of short, fluffy dark hair in the seat next to me. I suspected she was faking, but sooner rather than later, her soft regular breathing told me that she was out like a light.

I didn't usually find myself drawn to elves, and that was what she reminded me of. She couldn't have been an inch over 5'5, and her blue eyes were enormous and fringed with long dark lashes, giving her a gamine quality. That made her harasser's offense even worse somehow, and when she was asleep, I turned around quickly to make sure that I knew where he was sitting. He gave me a confused look, clearly having spotted me glaring at him earlier. And the guy hadn't actually done anything yet, so I couldn't blame him for wondering.

I sighed, leaning back in the seat. There was almost but not quite enough space for my legs under the seat in front of me, and again I cursed myself for not just renting a car in Chicago and driving up, though I hadn't taken the bus anywhere in close to ten years. Driving would have meant I'd get to the old homestead faster, however, and it would also mean I had nothing to do the whole drive besides being alone with my thoughts. When my mother had asked yet again about when I would be heading home, it had been convenient to tell her I was bound by the bus schedule, which we both knew was late more often than not.

Even through the phone, I could sense her disapproval, but she knew better than to try to start fighting with me so early in the game. She might have gotten somewhere doing that with David, but it would just make me hang up and skip everyone's calls for the next six months just like I'd done before. No, she would wait until I was at White Pines, and we were all gathered together like one big happy family before she started on the old song and dance with my father in chorus.

I wasn't looking forward to that at all, and I was grateful to Chloe for distracting me from my imminent future for at least a short while. When I glanced over, I saw that she had relaxed a little in her sleep. Now I could see her face, round and with just the barest dusting of dark freckles over her nose. Cute, I tried to tell myself, but that leap of heat when we had touched suggested some other words.

Goddamn, but you're a hypocrite, I told myself. I felt disgusted at the man who had driven her into my arms- uh, my seat- but sitting next to Chloe herself, I could feel a strange pull towards her, something that started at my heart and seemed to spread everywhere else. My thoughts were unruly enough that I wondered what it would be like to kiss her on her flushed cheek, just gently enough that she didn't wake up. Or perhaps she would wake up, and smile and...

And hopefully call the cops, I thought bitterly. *Jesus, but I'm an asshole sometimes.*

I could have passed it off as being a result of a long time between partners. Jennifer and I had gotten serious until she decided she needed someone more passionate, and Gail had been fun until I realized that she liked being a doctor's girlfriend more than she actually liked me. They were both tall, elegant, ambitious women, a lawyer and an installation artist respectively. They were my 'type,' insomuch as I had a type, but Chloe was blowing that idea to bits. She looked—and acted—like neither one of them, but I'd never felt a tug of desire quite as strong as that brief flash a few minutes back. I really didn't know what to do with it.

I grunted as something jostled my leg and watched with narrowed eyes as the man in the Packers jacket headed towards the front of the bus. He dropped a scrap of paper into the driver's trash bin and made his way back, avoiding my gaze but watching Chloe with that same hungry gaze that had startled her so badly. It was enough to make me want to deal with him right then and there, but just then, as if her sleep had been disturbed by his passing, Chloe whimpered, turned over, and buried herself against my side.

I froze for a moment, thinking that the best thing to do would be gently turn her back around, but then I relaxed into her embrace almost against my will. She was a soft warm weight against me, and now her arm came over my chest, pulling me closer still. She made a soft satisfied sound that was half enticing, half funny, and fell into a deeper sleep again.

I sighed, giving up any ideas of immediate vengeance and settled down instead against Chloe's sleeping form. She felt almost shockingly good against my side, and I reminded myself again that it was time to find another girlfriend. Maybe it was time for something a little different than the tall and elegant types I preferred.

Chloe didn't wear any perfume. The way her head was burrowed right underneath my chin, I could smell her shampoo, something bright and fruity, and underneath that was her own scent, soft and uniquely hers. She smelled like sleep and soap and home, and I couldn't help drifting off myself. At some point, it became natural to throw my arm over her shoulders, gathering her close as I leaned back in my seat to sleep.

I WOKE up to the bus drawing to a stop, and for a moment I thought we had slept all the way to White Pines. Instead, the driver announced a fifteen minute stop in Madison, and told us we were welcome to leave the bus as long as we were back in time. He apparently had no intention of keeping to the always-late creed. Damn.

Chloe must have been exhausted because she barely stirred at all before turning back to the window. I was momentarily disappointed to feel her warmth draw away, but as her harasser brushed past me again, I decided that it was just as well. Not bothering to put on my coat, I followed him off the bus and to the small shelter where he proceeded to pull out a cigarette.

He regarded me warily as I approached him, perhaps getting ready to defend himself with some kind of protestation that she hadn't minded all that much or even that he had been paying her a compliment. I had heard plenty of that kind of talk before; it was just as common at a hospital as it is elsewhere. There was no one at the shelter except for the two of us, everyone else choosing to run to the coffee shop across the street.

"Hey man, your girl, she's really cute, you know?"

The whine in his voice made my hackles rise, and I knew that I couldn't conceal the look of disgust that crossed my face.

"Don't get back on the bus."

He stared at me as if he wasn't sure that I was speaking English.

"What the hell, man..."

"I mean it. Don't get back on the bus. Stay here. Pass some time. There will be another bus here in three or four hours that runs the same route. Pay the driver and get on that one."

He started to get angry, his brows beetling at me and puffing up like a toad.

"Hey, you can't tell me what to fucking..."

I shrugged, because I had figured that there was a better than average chance it would come to this. As he stepped forward, so did I, and my forearm slammed across his collarbones. I pushed him back off of his feet and slammed him into the Plexiglas wall of the shelter with nothing more than a grunt of effort. He yelped, but then my forearm rolled up to his throat, threatening to cut off his air supply. He stared at me, and I smiled mirthlessly.

"I can threaten you with all sorts of things if you like," I said mildly. "I could call the police, I could refer you to the bus driver, I suppose, I could simply take it upon myself to get your name and start making life difficult for you..."

He looked supremely nervous at that, and I had the idea that he was wondering who I was and what I could actually do. It was less than what he thought, but his ignorance of the fact suited me just fine.

"... Or you can just call ahead to let your people know that you're going to be late, and take the second bus. Tell them you missed a connection or something. Then you never have to think about this again, and it all ends here."

I released him to see what he would do, and after a moment where it looked as if he might have wanted to fight, he nodded, two quick jerks of the head.

I nodded, because there was no need to humiliate him further, turned, and walked back to the bus. From the seat, I watched, and he never left the shelter, not even when the bus driver announced we were leaving.

Good riddance.

When the bus pulled away from the Madison stop, Chloe stirred a little, stretching out and looking around. Her bleary eyes told me that she would have far rather stayed asleep, and she gazed at me in some slight confusion, something that I found strangely endearing. I had to stop myself from reaching out to tuck a strand of dark hair behind her ear.

"What's going on?" she asked. "Are we in White Pines already?"

"No, we have another few hours yet. Go back to sleep."

"Oh, okay."

With nothing more than that, she snuggled up against me again, and this time, I didn't hesitate to wrap my arm around her. I told myself that there was nothing wrong with it, that people often leaned against each other on long bus rides, and that after all, she had started it.

I must have dozed off myself because suddenly my eyes opened, it was three hours later, and Chloe was stirring under my arm.

"Mm, feels nice," she murmured, but before she could enjoy herself too much, she came awake with a start, sitting up and drawing away. I was amused to see her cheek imprinted with the pattern of my sweater as she looked around in confusion.

"I am so, so sorry," she said contritely. "I didn't mean to sleep all over you like that..."

"No problem at all," I responded, stretching a little. "I got some sleep as well. No harm done."

She looked relieved at that and her shy smile zinged its way through me every bit as strong as the previous electric shock.

"Thank you for not minding and for everything, really. That bus trip could have been a lot nastier if you hadn't been here and so willing to give up the fun of sitting alone."

That was when we rolled into the small bus station at White Pines, and I realized that I might not be having much fun for a while. I put that out of my mind in favor of helping Chloe get put back together, and as we trundled to the front of the bus, she glanced behind her.

"Whatever happened to that guy who was bugging me?" she asked in confusion. I could have sworn he was sitting right back there.

"Lot of stops between here and northern Illinois," I responded with complete honesty. "He probably just got off while we were sleeping."

CHAPTER THREE

Chloe

I couldn't quite believe that I had managed to sleep all the way north from Illinois. Usually when I slept in the car, I ended up tossing and turning restlessly. Now, though, I felt as if I had finally caught up on some of the sleep I had lost last night and in the previous few weeks after learning about my pregnancy.

As we disembarked, I turned to Alex.

"Thank you again," I said. "I really mean it. And... I don't mean to be strange or forward or anything else that might offend your old man sensibilities..."

He raised an eyebrow at me.

"I'm thirty," he said.

"Well, you read a paper like an old man, anyway, but yeah, if it doesn't freak you out, maybe we could get together while I'm in town? I'm planning to be here for around a month or so."

He smiled at that and just as he was opening his mouth to reply, there was a flurry of motion off to one side.

"Oh Alex, there you are, I swear, we've been waiting forever and a day. I knew that you shouldn't have taken the bus..."

Instinctively, I stepped aside to make way for the woman in an actual fur coat to fly by me, throwing herself into Alex with a frenzy that reminded me of a feeding shark. She was tall, and Alex had her sandy hair. I realized I recognized her, and then with a start, I understood why.

She was Rina Reed, which meant that Alex was *that* Alexander Reed, part of one of the illustrious founding families of White Pines. Their money lay in the timber of the northern forests, and they were notoriously proud.

Alex looked as startled to see her as I was, and his expression quickly changed to something slightly mask-like and cool. Kind of like the way he'd looked when I first got on the bus, before he thawed.

"Mother, it's good to see you," he said with a slight trace of irony.

I might have kept on watching like a rude hick watching a prince, but then someone tapped me on the shoulder from behind. I turned to see two very familiar faces waiting behind me. Mara was tall with black hair like mine, but she wore it long and her eyes snapped with green fire. Shannon, born between us, looked as soft and warm as ever, her brown hair tucked under a bobble hat and her gray eyes warm.

It was Shannon that hugged me first, and for more than one reason, I fell into her arms, holding her tight. Our parents always said that she was the sweetest of the three of us, and after Mama and Dad died a few years ago, she was the one who made all the arrangements and kept us going with food and water when I might have collapsed and Mara would have worked herself into splinters.

"Oh, it's so good to see you, Chloe," she said, and I nodded against an unexpected lump in my throat. It had been almost two years since I had seen either of my sisters.

"If you've got that out of the way, I'm in a towaway zone," Mara said briskly. "Is that all you brought with you?"

Mara was dressed in a long black coat, and she looked as sharp as a knife. Just about everyone was at least a little intimidated by my big sister. She could be a little temperamental, but she'd come to my defense far too many times in the past for me to be too put off.

"Yeah, let's get going," I said with a grin. "Wouldn't want you to get a ticket on that shiny car of yours. I mean, I'm assuming it's still shiny."

Mara rolled her eyes at the tease. She was OCD about cleanliness in general, but when it came to her car—there better not be so much as a fingerprint on the hood or look out world! Didn't matter how many miles. Her wheels always shone.

As we walked to the small parking lot, I glanced behind me one last time to see Alex being hurried away by his mother and a younger man I figured must be his brother. We'd only spent a few hours together, but there was something in me that wrenched at the idea of being separated from him. It was idiotic, and I followed my sisters to Mara's gleaming car, which fortunately had not gotten a ticket. That would've been a great *welcome back*. Shannon gave me the front automatically because I always got carsick, and as she pulled out of the lot, Mara glared at the sky.

"It keeps threatening to snow, but refusing to," she said. "It needs to make up its mind..."

"Have you guys been back long?" I asked, and then I hesitated. "Have you been... to the place yet?"

Shannon shook her head, leaning back in the seat. She had come from farther than I had, and she looked worn out as well.

"I got in this morning, and Mara got in just an hour after I did. We've been grabbing some groceries to tide us over, talking with the lawyer..."

"What Shannon means is that no, we haven't been into Grandma's house yet," said Mara bluntly. "We wanted to wait for you. Do it all together."

She winced as if embarrassed to be caught in an obvious fib.

"We wanted to put it off," she said with a shrug. "Guess we can't any longer."

The drive to the little white house just four blocks away from the town center only took a few minutes, but we made the drive in silence. Of course it was Mara who led the way with her key in her hand, and she walked forward, unlocked the door after jimmying the rusted lock slightly, and flipped on the light automatically, like she'd done countless times.

"I had them turned back on," Mara explained automatically, before I could ask why the house had lights after being empty for so many years. "The water, too, since we'll be staying here at least a few days."

We crept into the house like invaders or thieves. I set my bag on the floor and then picked it up again awkwardly. The place echoed a little. A lot of the old decorations and knickknacks that once made it Grandma's house had been removed ages ago, leaving only the furniture. The fridge was unplugged with the door hanging open, and there were faded spots on the walls where the family pictures once had pride of place.

"I can't tell if it's better or worse that it looks nothing like what it used to look like," said Mara.

"It's different," said Shannon gazing around us. "It won't be what it was again, but that's not a bad thing at all."

"Yeah, I'm not going to miss the little dolls that Grandma collected. Didn't her great niece once removed get those? Those were creepy."

Shannon looked slightly scandalized, but Mara laughed.

"That's the spirit. We can't tiptoe around this place as if it was a shrine. Grandma's dead, and it's just a house now."

"Mara!" exclaimed Shannon, and Mara shook her head.

"Come on, Shannon. Grandma died more than five years ago. We're lucky that folks have been taking things out even before it made its way through probate. Less things for us to dig through."

Shannon blinked hard, and I suddenly realized that she was on the verge of tears. She had been the closest to Grandma, even thought we had all spent Christmas up at the house.

"That's just typical, Mara," she snapped. "You probably just want to gut this place so that you can go back to Atlanta."

Mara reared back as if she had been slapped. In a way, she had. Shannon had always been the peacemaker, the one soothing my fears and Mara's temper. For her to attack was more than a little strange.

"I'm trying to be sensible, Shannon," Mara said icily. "We're not here to spend Christmas together or to decorate a damn tree. We're here to look over the property, to decide what we want to do with it. This is a legal affair, not some kind of Christmas special."

"God, you're so freaking cold," Shannon said, throwing up her hands. "You're technically the one in charge as far as the papers go, I guess we're just lucky you didn't sell it out from under us."

"'Fucking,' Shannon, adults say fucking," said Mara, and I could tell that she was getting mean. God, she could get so mean sometimes, and suddenly I couldn't stand it any more. We'd squabbled and fought as much as any sisters did, but I couldn't take it while we were standing in Grandma's house, surrounded by old memories of when we had once been so happy together.

"I'm pregnant!"

It worked, or at least, Shannon and Mara turned to me with nearly identical expressions of shock and confusion. Mara looked as if I had sprouted wings and a tail, and a look of such longing passed over Shannon's face that I blinked.

"Like, with a baby?" said Mara slowly.

"Well, I hope it's not a puppy or a kitten?" I joked lamely.

Shannon crossed the floor to give me a hug. "Oh, Chloe." She pulled back to shake her head knowingly. "With Paul?"

"Er, Paul's out of the picture," I said with a half-shrug. "He knows, but he doesn't... um, want to be a part of things?"

Shannon made a concerned clucking noise, and Mara's eyes darkened.

"Blood tests and a court order when the baby's born," she said. "He has to take responsibility..."

"No!"

The sharp tone to my voice surprised everyone, including me. Being a mother-to-be was apparently making me unusually defensive.

"I don't want him involved," I explained. "Not after he decided that it might be anyone's baby."

Shannon and Mara made almost identical offended noises, and I nearly laughed at that.

"I'm going to be okay. It'll be tight, but there's that little alcove in my apartment, perfect for a crib, the library gives maternity leave, and there's a really nice lady in the building who looks after kids. I have a plan."

"There's more to taking care of a baby than..."

Shannon cleared her throat pointedly, and Mara nodded.

"All right. I think there's a decent crib up in the attic I can drive down for you, and when the time comes, I'll sign you up for a diaper service as a present. I did it for a co-worker at the magazine, and she liked it..."

Mara trailed off, shaking her head, and when she looked at me, some of the prickliness and anger had drained out of her.

"Shannon and I... we're going to be aunts," she said, and I

grinned as my grouchy older sister grudgingly hugged me and patted my flat belly with surprising tenderness. Just like that, the tension between the three of us died away.

All right, little one, well done, I thought. *Six months from being born and you're already quite the little problem solver.*

CHAPTER FOUR

lex

A I was around twelve when I first realized that the people of White Pines called our family's winter home 'Dracula's castle,' and heading up the long drive in Mother's Lamborghini reminded me of why. The place belonged to some several-times great grandfather who made all his money in lumber during the good times and whiskey during the bad, and it had more gables than any one residence should have. Three stories, eight bedrooms, more bathrooms, mullioned glass and a replica Victorian garden in the back; it was one of the most gorgeous houses around.

Of course I hated it.

Hate was a strong word, I supposed, but as we got closer, I started to feel the walls closing around me, even in the crisp and bright winter air. I had spent every winter in White Pines at this house until I turned eighteen and could finally beg off. This was my first year back, and it sounded like my mother was going to make the most of it

"And of course there's dinner with the Gannfields, and tomorrow, I was thinking a luncheon down at the country club, really show everyone that you're back. Of course I hope you packed something nicer than those rags, you ought to let Lupe throw them out. God, there's never been any good shopping here, but maybe we can send to that place your father likes in Chicago to have something delivered. Nothing much, but a good suit, some nice shirts."

I sighed, pulling my bag out of the car and stepping into the heated garage. David shot me an amused and sympathetic look. He had been home a little longer than I had been, but he'd never minded Mother as much.

"It's nice to see you too, Mother," I said, planting a careful kiss on her professionally made-up face. She brushed it aside, leading us toward the house, still talking when Father came out to greet us on the front step. Everyone said Father and I look alike, and with every year that passed, that grew more true. We were similarly tall, though his blond hair was a shade or two paler than mine, and his eyes stared into mine as if looking for anything else that we could possibly have in common. He'd never found anything, not as far as I knew, anyway.

"Good to see you," he said, formally shaking my hand. "Your hospital doing alright?"

"It's not my hospital at all, but my work is going well," I said pointedly. I'd always had the feeling that they would happily tell their friends that I was the hospital director or something like that if I'd let them get away with it. Having their firstborn son turn away from the family lumber business had been bad enough, but when I'd announced my decision to pursue a career as a trauma surgeon, it had nearly given them both heart attacks. You know, most families were actually *proud* of their kids who decided to grow up to be doctors ... heaven forbid the Reeds ever follow suit.

Father ignored my comment, shepherding all three of us into the breakfast nook for drinks. At least the drinks kept at Dracula's Castle tended to be better than average. I barely had time to look around at how exactly nothing had changed, when he started in.

"Did you think about that offer we talked about back in summer?" he asked as my mother worried at David's cuffs for some reason while my brother stood patiently waiting, as if he was five all over again.

"I did, and I told you my decision then," I said with a shrug. "Answer's still no, Dad."

He frowned.

"That's Reed money. It's not for frittering away on whatever fun you're having in Chicago."

I could already feel the tension headache threatening to descend. It was probably just as well that we were usually scattered to all ends of the earth for most of the year. If I had to live like this all the time, I'd be insane half the time and furious the rest.

"Last I checked, Great-Uncle Jim left me that money," I said, meeting my father eye to eye. "No riders or instructions to put it back into Reed lumber or anything like that."

My father glared, and he might have taken it farther- I almost wanted him to- but my mother descended.

"I need your measurements, Alex, I think I'll call the Chicago tailor now. With luck, we can get you some decent clothes for the luncheon. David tells me that the Lundorffs are going to be there, and their daughter Esme is visiting from school. She's a lovely girl, very sweet, majoring in education, isn't that nice? I'm sorry everything went belly up with that last girl you sent us a picture of, but you know, I never thought she was quite right for you.."

"Just based on the picture, Mother?" I asked, but she bulldozed straight ahead, plotting and planning right over me. That was familiar at least.

I shot David a dark look, and he grinned at me, shrugging slightly as he loosened his cuffs behind Mom's back.

Better you than me, his look said, and obviously that hadn't changed either.

"Alex dear, you're what, twenty-four, twenty-five? It's long past time for you to find someone nice, settle down a bit..."

"I'm thirty, Mother," I said, and she shook her head in denial of my age as she had for the last five years or so, refusing to admit she'd given birth to me that long ago. Any sign of age for Mom was a no-go, even if it meant pretending she couldn't remember her son's birthday.

"Oh surely not," she scoffed. "Argue with me all you like, but you can't tell me that your life wouldn't be a little happier and a little brighter with a sweet girl at your side, especially one as lovely and well-connected as Esme Lundorff..."

She was off again, and no one really had to add anything to keep the conversation going so we stood around in awkward silence. What she said stuck with me, as a girl I didn't know brought us a tray of snacks from the kitchen.

When I thought of a sweet girl, I certainly didn't think of Esme, who had been known as a little girl for cutting off other girls' braids. Instead I thought of bright blue eyes and a fluff of dark hair, cheeks pink in the cold and a sassy mouth that just begged to be kissed.

Wherever you are, Chloe, I hope you're having a better time with this than I am...

I HAD MADE plans to stay up in White Pines for two weeks, skipping out on the actual Christmas celebration in favor of being back in Chicago. The actual holidays were a bad time for the trauma ward, and I had much more loyalty to my patients and my staff than I did to my family, who couldn't be bothered with any loyalty to me.

Two days, drinks, a luncheon, a party and a family talk about how dirty Chicago was, and I had no idea how I was going to make it a week, let alone three. I might have taken off to go on a roaring bender with my brother, but David had actually somehow hit it off with Esme Lundorff- now tall and slender, it turned out, and no longer quite so inclined to cut other women's hair- and they were spending all their time in the indoor squash court. On his way past with his racket, however, David had poked his head into the library.

"Mother wants you to escort her to some kind of winter garden party viewing this afternoon. She says she's expecting you in something festive. Fair warning."

I sighed. I could plant my feet, say I wasn't going to go, start a fight. Win or lose though, it would be unpleasant, and right then, it seemed far better to simply be impossible to locate. I pulled on the wool coat that I had worn up from Chicago and a battered pair of old boots that I found at the back of my closet and headed off into the woods instead.

The family house backed onto the Snake River, which circled about half of White Pines. Farther south, it slowed to a trickle and joined the Mississippi, but up in White Pines, it was a steady torrent.

The other side of the river was a national forest, but the side closest to town sported a thick fringe of woods and a pleasant, if slightly primitive, path along the water. The path was a little more run-down than I remembered it being, but it suited my mood just fine. I picked my way along the water and let my mind clear of everything, family included. It must have been a mile or more before I heard the shuffle of steps coming towards me, and then there was a girl walking around the bend. She was small enough to be a teenager, but I immediately recognized her blue coat, the same one that had snuggled up to me on the bus ride. It was nearly the same color as her eyes, and the knit yellow hat she wore over it was like a little spot of sun in the gray day.

"Chloe!"

She looked up at my greeting, and I got a flash of those bright blue eyes right before she missed her step and tumbled right off of the path. With a curse, I lunged forward and grabbed her arm before she tumbled down the long slope that led to the water below. Not soon enough to keep her from falling to her knees on the leaf-strewn ground, however.

"Oh God, give a girl some warning!" she gasped, her eyes huge with surprise, and I shot her a wry look.

"I thought I had, actually."

I set her upright once more and looked her over quickly. She looked fine, but I found myself strangely reluctant to get away. She looked up at me, her cheeks reddened with the cold, her lips slightly parted with the exertion of the fall, and I felt that same surge of electricity go through me again. It would be so easy to kiss her here, but my instincts as a doctor kicked in instead. Those instincts also kept me from automatically reaching out to dust leaves off her, thereby putting my hands all over her.

"Here. I'm going to hang on to you, and I want you to try to take a few steps, all right?"

Chloe did as I said, and when she put her weight on her left foot, she staggered a little.

"Hmm, sprained maybe," I said, but she shook her head.

"It's fine, it doesn't matter..."

"It really does, we should get you to a..."

"Could that have hurt my baby?"

I froze, caught as off guard as she had been a minute earlier. There were a dozen questions running through my head, but right now, hers was the most important one.

"Unlikely, but it's possible," I said at last. "If you're pregnant, we should definitely get to the hospital. They can tell you for sure what's going on."

She nodded bravely, but i could see the concealed panic in her eyes. She might be twenty-four, but there was something unusually sweet and innocent in her eyes, unjaded, something that made me want to comfort her.

"We should be safe, but you're probably fine. You didn't fall that far, and you didn't hit anything hard."

Chloe found a grin for me, bright and nearly dizzying.

"You saved me," she said softly. "Thank you."

Her thanks filled me with a warmth I really didn't care to look at too closely. Instead I looked up and down the path.

"Did you drive here?"

She nodded.

"My sister's car is just a few minutes back that way."

"Good. That's short enough that a piggyback ride is probably our best bet."

When she started to protest, I gave her an impatient look.

"The sooner we get to the hospital, the sooner you can confirm that everything's all right. You're hardly going to break my back."

She gave me a dubious look, but reluctantly, she consented to climb up on my back, and I set off in the direction she indicated.

"You must be a nurse," she said after a moment, and I stifled a laugh as I kept walking. She was a light but dense warmth over my back, and with her arms wrapped so trustingly around me, it all felt strangely right. Arousal danced through me at the feel of her warm body pressed into mine, but alongside it was something more. Something atypically peaceful and content.

"Why do you say that?"

"Because nurses are the ones who care," she said promptly.

"I'm pretty sure a doctor would have just told me to get to the hospital."

"I'd argue with you, but I've known too many doctors," I quipped. "Sorry to disappoint, but I am a doctor. Trauma medicine though, and hopefully that keeps me from being too terrible."

"Oh!" she exclaimed. "God, what was I thinking. I'd forgotten you're a Reed. I guess you wouldn't be a nurse, would you?"

It was close enough to something my father had said when I decided on medical school, something about being no better than a nurse, that I had to blink.

"I think I would make a pretty good nurse," I said offhandedly, and somehow, she must have sensed that there was some kind of disquiet there because her arms tightened around my shoulders, and she nuzzled me like a cat. It sent a bolt of sensation through me when she somehow found a bit of bare skin beyond the collar of my coat, and I wondered if she could feel the way that I shook a little.

"I know you would have been a great nurse, and I bet you're an awesome doctor," she said, soundly oddly loyal, and I had to laugh.

"I like to think I do alright."

Her sister's car was an exquisitely well-maintained Mercedes, and I was grateful for the size when I loaded Chloe into the passenger's seat. I ignored her protestations that she could drive, and pulled out onto the road.

"Should I call someone, let them know where you are?"

"Oh God no," Chloe said with a shudder. "Mara and Shannon are already going to be upset that I took off without telling anyone, and when it comes out that I almost hurt myself, I'll never hear the end of it..."

"Well, I meant your husband or boyfriend..."

She shot me an amused glance from the passenger seat.

"So sure it's a husband or a boyfriend? I mean, I might have a wife or a girlfriend..."

The thought hadn't actually crossed my mind, and when it did, it ended up being an image of Chloe, pretty naked Chloe, wrapped around another beautiful woman, and I banished it immediately because God, I could not be that kind of asshole. Could I?

"Do you?"

She laughed at me, and the sound, soft and bell-like, made me smile like nothing else had in the past two days.

"No, but I think you're blushing. I thought Reeds were way too well-bred to blush..."

"Yes, most of my family is actually made of marble. The only reason I can blush is because of a great-aunt made of ruby on my mother's side..."

She giggled a little bit at that, and I thought all over again about how much I liked that sound.

"Anyway, sass and blushing all aside, is there anyone you want me to call?"

Chloe looked down at that, not in shame, I realized, but out of thoughtfulness.

"No," she decided firmly. "I'll call my sisters later, but aside from them, there's no one that needs to know."

"That sounds like there's a story there."

"A dumb one, maybe. I was seeing a guy at home, Paul. He was nice enough, but I guess it was one of those situations where it turns out I was way more into him than he was in to me. I think he might have cheated on me a few times. Anyway. I got pregnant, he blew up and said that it could have been anyone's. I honestly thought that that would have broken my heart, but after he stormed out... I felt relief. Do you think that makes me awful?"

"I don't think anything could make you awful." I found that I was surprisingly serious about that, but she laughed and continued.

"Well, I guess I wasn't into him as much as I thought I was. What I felt for him, it was like a candlelight that could blow out when a door slammed. But what I feel for this little one..."

She glanced down at her belly where she had laid her hands. There was something so tender and loving about how she gazed at her future child that I had to drag my attention back to the road. It made my heart beat a little faster, made me long for something that I wasn't sure I had words for. I was suddenly certain that she had the words, though, and in the back of my mind, I wondered if she would teach me.

"The love is a tower of fire, and I know it's never going to go out."

She said the words simply and sincerely, and I could tell she meant them to the bottom of her heart.

"Then he or she is going to be lucky indeed," I said quietly.

When we got to the hospital, it was quiet, and someone came to see us relatively soon. Patient had never been my middle name, and I'd become even more prone to impatience during my years in the city, it seemed, because it felt as if everything was moving as if it was stuck in tar. Nurses were slow, the doctor was occupied, and I was feeling more and more tightly wound until Chloe put a small hand on my own.

"Don't worry," she said. "The nurse said that there was no overt sign of trauma. Everything after this is just details."

For a moment, I wanted to pull away and run down the doctor myself if I had to, but I knew that she was right. I sat on the hard plastic chair next to her, and surprisingly, she didn't let go of my hand. Her small fingers laced through mine and I didn't hesitate to wrap my own around them. She didn't sleep, but she closed her eyes, resting quietly until someone could come to see us. I found myself wishing she'd lean into me, like on the bus, but she didn't.

"I really know how to show a guy a good time, don't I?" she murmured without opening her eyes. "For my next trick, I'll make you take Mara's car to the car wash."

"Well, I think you can do better than that," I said with a slight grin. "Maybe give it a try?"

She opened her eyes just a little, the blue a slight sparkle.

"Gas station sandwiches?"

"No..."

"Winter time petting zoo?"

"No."

She paused for a moment, and when she spoke again, her voice was soft and serious, no joke in it at all.

"There's...a star shower tomorrow night. The Geminids. We could go to see that. I'll bring hot chocolate."

"I would love to," I said, and I brought her hand up to kiss it. I meant it to be light and playful, but that electricity shocked us again. This time, there was no bus full of people to see or an injury to tend to. Her eyes were wide as I reached out to touch her face, but she didn't resist as I moved closer...

"Miss Becker?"

We pulled apart like two guilty teenagers, and for a minute, I had a very satisfying image of simply pushing the doctor out of the room and barricading the door.

Instead I listened as he gave Chloe the usual cautions, told her to bind up the ankle, to use heat for pain relief, and cold to bring down the swelling. He did an exam that I stepped out for, and when I was called back in he told us both that there was no sign that any harm had come to her baby, but if she noticed anything unusual, she should come back in. Otherwise, she was free to go. Chloe flopped back on the exam table with a sigh of relief as he left.

"I'm glad you said yes to the date," she said softly. "I'm really glad..."

She never got to say what she was glad about, because the door opened and her two sisters stalked in. It was fascinating. There was a family resemblance, especially around the nose and the shape of the mouth, but otherwise, all three Becker sisters were totally different.

"No injuries?" asked the tallest one, her eyes as sharp and shrewd as Chloe's were soft and gentle. She gave me an appraising glare.

Chloe rolled her eyes.

"No, Mara. I'm fine, the baby's fine. Alex was kind and got to me almost immediately."

The other sister turned to me with a slight smile that took her from plain to surprisingly lovely. "Thank you so much for looking after Chloe..."

"And now we're going to talk about you taking my keys and my car, not leaving a note, and ignoring your phone," Mara said with deadly purpose, and I almost started laughing. Chloe shot me a despairing look.

"Thank you for your help, Alex," she said helplessly. "It looks like my sisters have got it from here. Run, run while you still can."

Despite her position, I could almost see the strong bonds of love that held the three sisters together. It was so different from the strained and bitter strings running between myself and my own family that it was like a punch in the gut.

"See you tomorrow night," I said, and reluctantly, I walked out.

CHAPTER FIVE

Chloe

I was happy that Alex didn't seem to have any macho hangups about letting me drive that night. It turned out that I knew White Pines and the surrounding countryside better than he did, and after a discussion about When We Can And Can't Take Mara's Car and Look What Happened When We Didn't Know Where You Were; You Could Have DIED, Mara ultimately let me abscond with her precious Mercedes. But not before Bring It Back In the Same Condition You Borrowed It!

Of course driving up to the Reed house, I was suddenly reminded of what all the kids had called it years ago. It really did look like Dracula's castle rising up out of the forested landscape, and I felt just a little like a human sacrifice as I left the safety of Mara's Mercedes and went to ring the bell.

A narrow woman in an expensive-looking sweater and black slacks opened the door, diamond earrings glinting demurely at her ears and a bright, very definitely fake smile on her face.

"Oh you must Chloe," she said, her voice just a shade too brittle. "Alex will be right down."

Instead of letting me step into the house to get out of the late-night chill, however, she only looked me up and down.

"So you're from town?" she asked.

"Oh, no, Mrs. Reed, though we used to spend vacations here. My grandma lived in town though, and we came to visit all the time..."

"Oh I see," she said. "And where did you come from? Alex said that you were on the bus with him."

From the tone of disgust in her voice, I could imagine what she thought of the bus, and I couldn't help shuffling a little.

"Oh, I'm from this little town just outside of the suburbs, Havenwoods. I work at the library there, we have this amazing program for kids that are slow to read. The school district has had some rough times, and this project really gets kids invested in reading..."

I knew that I was babbling, but I couldn't stop myself. Under her sharp eye, I felt as if every piece of me was under scrutiny and nothing was passing muster at all.

"How nice," she said a little sharply. "Alex is of course a doctor in Chicago."

"Yes, I know," I stammered. "I mean, I know because he—"

Before I could make a further fool of myself, Alex appeared, looking almost achingly handsome in a dark coat and dark jeans and boots. He smiled at me for a moment before shooting a grimly amused glance at his mother.

"Why Mother, for a second there it almost sounded like you were proud of my chosen career path," he said dryly. He led me back out before she had a chance to respond, and in just a few minutes, we were on the road again, with me behind the wheel this time.

"Er, so your mom doesn't like the idea of you being a doctor?"

He shot me an amused look that still didn't manage to hide a hint of real frustration and pain.

"It's a bit of an old and tired story, but yes. I didn't even have the self-respect or family loyalty to go into anything like research or cardiology. The Reeds did not expect to have a son who liked mucking around in trauma wards."

"I'm just going to be proud if my kids decide they want to save lives," I declared, focusing on the dark road in front of me. "Doesn't matter to me how they want to do it."

I jumped a little bit when Alex reached over to touch my shoulder gently. There it was again, that rich warmth that passed between us, and I remembered how close we had come to kissing at the damned hospital. I loved Mara and Shannon, but I could have smacked them both for coming in when they did. Of course they had both laughed their heads off when I told them that, but the point stood.

"I think you're going to be a good mother," he said, and the unusual softness to his tone left me halfway to melting.

"Thanks," I said. "Sometimes... I worry about it."

Before we could get into the many hundreds of fears I had about being a single mother, I saw our turn up ahead.

"This driveway leads about a mile back into the fields and woods to an old foundation. No one's got any reasons to use the foundation at all, so it ought to be great for us."

I pulled the car over in a small field, and as Alex watched in bemusement, I pulled an old quilt out of the trunk of the car and spread it on the ground. Our breath was steaming in the air, but it wouldn't be too bad, I thought.

After watching for a moment, Alex stretched out on his back next to me, and as if we always did this, he reached out to take my hand.

"This is adorable," he chuckled, and I bristled a little bit.

"Look, I'm sorry if this isn't as exciting as all the nightclubs and soirees in Chicago..."

"The closest I get to Chicago nightlife is when there's a

shooting at a club and I need to patch people up," he said with a laugh. "This is wonderful."

I would have responded with something snarky, but then a yellow streak crossed the sky, so fast that it would have been lost if I blinked.

"Oh, I saw one!" I yelped, pointing up at the sky with my free hand, and Alex turned.

"I think you're fibbing," he started to say, but then we saw the next one, bright, vivid and gone in a heartbeat.

It was the peak of the Geminids, with one or more falling stars every minute, and we watched them in rapt silence, only exclaiming when we saw one that was particularly bright.

As we watched, I became strangely aware of Alex next to me. It was as if there were magnets within us, dragging us together through the sheer natural force of gravity. It was inevitable, and fighting it felt like the worst kind of nonsense. Somehow, I had grown closer to him over the last half hour, my hip pressed to his, my ankle knocking against his. Or perhaps he had grown closer to me?

When I glanced over at him, I realized he had been watching me for a while. In the dark, it was impossible to read his expression, but I could feel the hunger radiating from him, hunger and need and something almost wistful.

"You're brighter than any star in the damn sky," he muttered, and it was so cheesy that he flushed, but also so obviously sincere that I couldn't have kept myself from kissing him just then if my sisters or even aliens had dropped down in the field beside us.

I pulled him over me, leaning up to brush my lips over is. It was electricity and heat, sweet and lovely, and then he came over me again, his mouth hot and more insistent this time. He carefully held his weight over me, leaning on his elbows so he wouldn't crush me, but the kiss was consuming and claiming.

When I felt his tongue trailing along my lower lip, I opened my mouth and gave him the entrance he was craving.

"You taste even sweeter than you look," Alex whispered, framing my face with his big hands.

I felt overwhelmed with the power of him and the heat of our bodies together. He kissed me for a timeless moment, and then his mouth trailed down to my throat, tugging my scarf aside so he could get to the warm skin there. I moaned in surprise at the sudden pleasure of his lips pressed against such sensitive skin, and that small sound only seemed to encourage him all the more. He returned to ravishing my mouth as his hand worked at the buttons of my coat.

"Dammit, it's freezing out here," he swore suddenly, hands stilling.

"Well, winter in Wisconsin," I said. "Alex, I don't want you to stop..."

For a second, I thought I had convinced him. I had a flurry of images of us making love here in the open, under the falling stars... struggling with my coat and his, deciding which bits we could afford to have frozen off, which we still needed, and then he shook his head.

"If we ever want to try this outside again, I'll think about some kind of tropical getaway," he growled. "This is too damn cold. Come on, pretty girl."

He swiftly refastened my coat and pulled me to my feet. For a brief moment, I thought that we were just going to say goodnight, but then he pulled me in for another quick hard kiss.

"Where can we go?" he asked. "You know White Pines better than I do..."

"I'll take you to my place," I said, and as we got back into the car, I wondered why that single line made my heart skip a beat.

∽

THE HOUSE WAS quiet and dark when we got back. I remembered belatedly that my sisters had decided to go to an art night in White Pines' tiny downtown. Despite how dark it already was, it wasn't too late, and they probably weren't back yet.

Alex looked around the house curiously as I led him up to the tiny attic room that had always been mine when we came to stay as teenagers, but he didn't say anything until the door was closed behind us.

"Nice place," he said, looking around. It was almost spartan, only containing some bookshelves, two dressers and the narrow iron bed that I had slept in since I was a girl. I was suddenly glad that someone had gotten the random rack of dolls out of the place. I had liked them when I was little, but now, about to hopefully have sex with the most handsome man I had ever known, I was pleased that they were gone.

Now that we were alone in this warm place, however, I suddenly felt awkward. I fumbled with the buttons on my plaid shirt, feeling unnervingly awkward and young, and I could feel myself blushing as I swore.

Alex chuckled, but before I could even get embarrassed that he was making fun of me, he drew me close again. When he kissed me, I forgot about everything. There was nothing more important than feeling the warmth of his mouth, the press of his body against mine and the way his breath fanned my cheek.

"Hey," he said, smiling into my eyes. "No need to be nervous, all right? This is good. I'm going to make you feel so good."

I started to respond to that, but then his long clever fingers - surgeon's hands, I thought hazily- were unbuttoning my shirt. He moved quickly, but when the shirt hung open, he took his time easing it down off of my shoulders. When it fell to the ground he looked at me solemnly in the light of the moon that came in the window. I resisted the urge to cover myself; Paul had always said that I was shaped like a fourteen year old boy, but when I looked at Alex's face, I could see nothing but desire and pleasure at looking at me.

"God but you're beautiful," he murmured, and he stepped closer, burying his face in the crook of my neck. For a moment, we simply breathed each other in, but then he started kissing me, running a line of kisses down my throat to my suddenly surprisingly sensitive collarbones. I felt him fumbling briefly with the clasp of my bra, and then in another moment, it was gone too. The bra joined the shirt on the floor, and then I was naked to the waist.

"So very perfect," he purred, and he reached down to gently touch one erect nipple and then the other. I gasped a little, leaning in to his touch. I had always thought that having small breasts was a fault, but now when he was sending sensations racing through me with just a touch, I knew I would never think that again.

"I think I need to see all of you," he said gravely, and I couldn't help giggling at that.

"Oh really, doctor? Do you think it's serious?"

I surprised a laugh out of him, and he grabbed me up in a hug that seemed to pull out all the darkness inside me, replacing it with light.

"God, but you can be just a brat," he murmured tenderly.

"Oh well, if that's all..." I yelped in surprise when he dropped me on the bed. Instead of joining me, however, he started to work on my jeans, working them and my panties down my hips. I lifted myself up a little to help him, but he pushed me back down. When I was naked in front of him, he simply stood by the side of the bed and gazed at me. I felt as if I was someone else, someone beautiful and rare and precious.

"I want to see you too..." I said, stammering a little. It was true though. I didn't think that I could go much longer without touching his face, without seeing him as bare as I was.

He nodded, and with far less ceremony, started stripping out of his clothes. He moved with a kind of efficiency that made me smile, and then his clothes were in an untidy pile on the floor, and he stood in front of me. He was handsome clothed, but naked there was something vital about him, something almost primal. He was lean but well-muscled, and without thinking, I reached out to run a gentle finger from the curve of his shoulder, down his chest to the corrugated muscle over his belly. There was a thin trail of pale hair there, and I followed it down to his cock, which was more than half-hard already.

He came to rest next to me on the bed. It was a little too short for him and really not wide enough for two people, but we made it work by pressing hard against each other. The shared warmth felt like the most wonderful kind of pleasure, and then he started to kiss me again, one hand running smoothly down my side to my hip and my thighs.

I gave myself up to the kiss. There was no hurry to him at all. There was the urgency of his cock pressed against me, the fine tension that was strung through his frame, but there was nothing impatient about his motions. He seemed content to take his time, as if he would be happy doing nothing more than kissing me, and that drew a shiver of pleasure through my body.

At first I was content to be kissed, but then I couldn't help touching him back. I learned the textures of his body, the smooth and rough parts, how he would purr when I knitted my fingernails into his chest. When I reached down between us to tentatively circle his cock with my hand, he gasped a little, pressing against me. I liked the needy sound he made, and I drew my hand over his cock, marveling at the soft skin over the hard flesh. It drew an answering pulse from deep inside me. When I felt a bead of liquid at the very tip of his member, I swirled it over the head, making him bite back a groan.

"God, you're going to undo me..." Alex breathed in my ear,

sending a tickle down my spine. He didn't miss that, and with a growl, he pinned me underneath him.

"Do you like that?" he growled, his breath warming the sensitive skin there. "Does this feel good, pretty?"

His sharp teeth snapped lightly at my earlobe, and I couldn't believe how it made me shiver. It was as if my spine had been replaced with lightning from that single comparatively gentle touch, and I gasped, clinging to him, my eyes wide.

"Feels good," I echoed, and then he nibbled at the rim of my ear as his hand slid down my body. He slid warm fingertips along my slit, finding my wet warmth, and just as he touched my clit, he ran his teeth over my earlobe again.

I cut off a full-throated cry because it rocked my entire body. It felt as if every nerve I had was set on fire, and of course, Alex kept doing it. He lapped at the new-found sensitive skin of my ear, he slid a firm finger over my clit and then deep inside me. I could feel tension building up inside me, higher and higher. Where before I had always had to work on that tension, to nurture it and to help it grow, this time, it simply happened, taking me along for the ride.

"Oh please, please," I murmured, and the sound he made was more a groan than a laugh. His fully hard cock pressed hard against my hip, and I wanted him more than anything.

Just as I was trembling on the edge of a climax, he pulled away. I let out a cry of shocked need, but instead he rolled on top of me, pressing me back to the bed. His mouth claimed mine with a kind of ferocity that took my breath away, and then he was pressing my thighs apart. He slid the tip of his cock over my slit, nudging my clit and teasing the entrance until I could barely stand it any more.

"Alex, please, I can't wait," I said, just a hair away from begging.

"Neither can I," he murmured, and then he slid his cock fully inside me. I sheathed him on that first stroke, and for a moment, we simply stared each other in wonder at how good it felt. Then he started to move, and I dug my fingernails into his shoulders, hanging on for dear life.

With every stroke, the pleasure in me roared higher. Somewhere underneath it all, I could feel that he was still watching me, still making sure that I felt good and that I would be alright. He needn't have worried. It felt as if my body had been set aflame, and now I was roaring high up into the sky, ready to meet those falling stars.

My climax rose and rose, but somehow when it broke, it still caught me with surprise. I threw my head back on the pillow, crying out in shock and surprise and pleasure. I felt like a fireworks show, the sweetness of my climax bursting over and over again until I was exhausted.

My climax triggered Alex's, and I could distantly feel his strokes become faster, less rhythmic. Just as I was relaxing into the bed, I felt him spill inside me, growling against my shoulder as he did so. I could feel every part of him, and we were joined in the most intimate way possible. As we relaxed, I threw my arms around him, needing him close. It was a perfect warmth and everything felt almost painfully good.

Alex pulled away slightly, enough so that he could roll to his side and gather me in his arms. We lay like that so long that I nearly fell asleep, and then he stirred.

"We should get under the covers," he said, and I smiled at his practicality.

"Are you just inviting yourself to stay the night?" I asked, and he paused, considering.

"Should I not?"

"No, I want you to stay. I'm just being a brat. It got such good results before."

He growled playfully at me, but he still covered me with the blanket, letting me nestle next to him. The bed was really far too small for two people, especially when one of them was as large as Alex, but right then, nothing in the world mattered at all except being close to each other. We drifted off to sleep in each others arms, and when his hand drifted over my belly, I smiled.

CHAPTER SIX

Alex

The next morning felt like a continuation of some kind of dream. Chloe woke me with tiny kisses peppered across my jaw, and then we made love like giddy teenagers, tripping over each other in the tiny shower and kissing each other's cries silent so her sisters wouldn't hear, although they more than likely at least heard the various shampoo bottles being dropped everywhere. But even when the low, rusty shower head tried to decapitate me, and even when a razor went flying and almost took off a piece of my bicep, and even when the biggest damn shampoo bottle I'd ever seen landed squarely on my instep, none of that mattered because Chloe was in my arms, moaning my name. Chloe was pressed to my chest, legs wrapped tightly around me, her face buried in my neck as she came violently, triggering my own fierce climax.

There was no need to think of protection for the first time in my life—we both automatically knew we were clean, plus, her pregnancy—and spilling deep inside Chloe felt like nothing else ever had, or, I suspected, ever would again.

When we finally unwrapped from one another and snuck

out of the shower, making a dead run for the bedroom and laughing hysterically at the absurdity of adults acting like total kids, it struck me hard that I was more than halfway to being in love with this woman already. This woman I barely knew, but who somehow fit exactly right into my arms and heart and life.

And then that gorgeous, sweet, sexy woman kicked me out.

"Sorry," Chloe said apologetically, handing me my pants just when I was about to tumble her into bed once more.

I froze in confusion and she laughed, leaning in to steal a quick kiss. "Don't look like that." She rested her forehead against mine, beautiful eyes twinkling. "But my sisters will only give us so much leeway before they decide they're entitled to emerge from their rooms for breakfast …"

Chuckling, I held up my hands in surrender, even though they wanted to reach for her bare body, still deliciously warm and damp from the shower. "Okay, okay. I know when I'm not wanted."

Reaching for her own clothes, Chloe shot me a hungry look that almost undid me right then and there. "Oh, you're wanted. And if we have to get a hotel next time so you don't have to leave, we will."

Then she smiled and handed me a phone to call a cab, but it was fine because she'd said *next time*.

MY PARENTS WERE STILL ASLEEP when I slipped into the house, but David was fresh from a workout in the small gym in the basement. He saluted me with a glass of something green and unpleasant-looking.

"You look like you had a good night."

"I did," I said with a smile. I had no intention of sharing any details with him, but I didn't see the harm in agreeing.

"That's one of the Becker girls, isn't it? Mother was talking about her last night. Someone mentioned that they were back in town."

There was nothing intrinsically wrong with my brother's words, but something about his tone made me scowl.

"Yes, she is. They're here to decide on what they want to do with their grandmother's house."

David chuckled, and it occurred to me how very far apart we were. He was almost ten years younger than me, and for a good chunk of the time he was growing up, I was in medical school.

"White Pines girls are great," he said. "Townie girls. They think going down to Madison is like being taken to Paris, they don't mind slumming it in parked cars, and they think that if you get them dinner at that greasy burger place on Shaw that you're really into them. Good for a cheap night out."

I stared at him for a moment, wondering when my father's voice had suddenly started coming out of David's mouth.

"Are you serious?" I asked, and he laughed.

"Hey, I love them," he said. "I have ever since I stopped worrying about cooties. White Pines occasionally throws a looker, and it sounds like from how mad Mom is that you got a pretty one. Works for me, I like Esme just fine."

He threw a quick salute at me before heading for the shower. He had a date with Esme that day and he needed to look his best, but suddenly I thought that I would much prefer him with a black eye or maybe a split lip.

He's just joking, I told myself. *David's barely more than a kid, and he says all sorts of dumb shit.* It was a cruel thing to say, and I wasn't used to my brother being cruel.

Or maybe he was and you just never noticed...

I stripped in my bedroom and when I saw the small red marks that her nails had left behind, I smiled, touching them a little, and the tension slipped away just like that. Sex with Chloe was extraordinary, but what was even more amazing was that I wanted way more than that with her. The way I wanted … everything.

As I was changing into clean clothes, my phone buzzed. I glanced at it, hoping it was Chloe. Weirdly, it was David.

"Why is my brother texting me when we're in the same house?" I said to no one in particular, reading the message.

Esme's hot, right? I'm not slumming?

The realization that my brother really was the jerk he appeared to be made me faintly sick.

She's gorgeous. I answered. *And you're an ass.*

Really? I'm not too good for her?

Man, she is way too good for you, I texted back wearily. *When did you mutate, Dave?*

So you don't see Chloe as slumming?

I was so livid that I hit send before my thumbs finished tripping over themselves. *Unlike your feelings toward Esme, I'm too good for her.*

Told you …

That's not what I meant! I'm not *too good for her. Chloe is amazing. And if Esme is as smart as I remember her being, she'll run screaming from you.*

Esme's mean. I like em that way.

He stopped texting at that point and I was glad, because I was ready to track him down and break his face.

After changing into clean clothes, I decided to borrow one of the cars in the garage, head to town, and look for a present for Chloe. It somehow seemed like the least I could do when my family was just so utterly clueless about how great she was.

Before I could get very far, however, my mother buttonholed me in the den, smiling in a determined way that made me immediately wary.

"It's so nice to have you home again," she said. "I don't know if I've told you that yet..."

"Actually, no, you haven't. You never do," I said wryly, but she bulldozed ahead as if I hadn't said anything.

"And the holidays are just an amazing time for family, aren't they? It's a wonderful time to remember who's really important and to let what's not important fall to the wayside. It's so easy to get distracted during the year..."

"Is there a point to this?" I asked, and she shot me an exasperated look.

"I just wanted to make sure that you were fully aware of the holiday party on Friday. You can be a sly one, Alex, and I don't want to get to the day and find out that you somehow forgot or that you slipped off to go stargazing or some nonsense. There are people attending who haven't seen you in years, and your father and I have had to make excuses for you for too long."

She looked at me expectantly, and reluctantly I nodded. I had never been a huge fan of my family's stuffy holiday parties. They were full of people who liked nothing better than to show off how much better they were than the rest of the world, how much richer, better educated and intelligent they were. Medicine, at least trauma medicine, was a great equalizer, and it made these get-togethers increasingly grating. Still, I was in White Pines ostensibly to see my family ...

"Fine, I'll be there," I said with a sigh, and she nodded, apparently satisfied. As I turned to go, however, I saw her narrow her eyes at me, as if uncertain or frustrated with something I couldn't see. I didn't ask. She could bring it up, or we could ignore it.

Downtown White Pines was unexpectedly busy for a weekday afternoon. It was a rustic spot, but there were plenty of small artisan shops, and people were obviously shopping for the holidays. I was just on my way to the town's only flower shop when my phone rang.

"Hi! So, I don't know if it's okay to call you? We had sex... so at least we should be on texting terms, I think..."

7
CHAPTER SEVEN

Chloe

Thank God, he chuckled at my rambling. I stretched out on my bed in my clean clothes, on the same sheets Alex and I had made love on, and grinned from ear to ear.

"Well, given how we spent last night," he drawled. "I would say that we're definitely on texting terms. Hell, I might even be so bold as to suggest we're way past that."

"I thought I probably shouldn't call you," I admitted, simply because telling Alex anything that came to mind felt oddly natural. "You know. Because."

"I don't know," he replied. "Why shouldn't you call me? People on beyond-texting-terms should definitely call each other constantly."

The grin stretched further yet, making my face ache. "Because I don't want to come across as needy."

He growled a little and I swear I damn near swooned.

"I like you needy. You should always be needy for me, Chloe. Doesn't matter if I've known you five minutes or seen you two seconds back. You needing me makes me close to insane."

I am in so much trouble, I thought to myself.

"Alex, we've honestly only known each other two seconds—"

He cut me off. "And those two seconds have meant more than two years I've spent with previous women. I mean it, Chloe. It's insane, I admit, but I'm all in. 100% in, baby. Are you?"

I bolted upright in bed, hand resting over my stomach. "Yes. Yes, I am, Alex, my God, yes! But, the bab—"

"Meet me at Malarky's on Shaw," he interrupted. "Soon as you can. I'll be waiting. Don't leave me out in the cold too long, honey."

I FLEW TO MALARKY'S. Honestly, I don't think the cab's tires even touched the road once. I shoved money at the cabbie and tumbled out, looking around until I spotted Alex perched on what was probably a frigid bench.

He saw me at the exact same moment I saw him, and then that movie moment thing happened between us again when his eyes met mine.

Alex walked up to me and held out a single red rose, framed by baby's breath. "For you," he said simply, then drew me into his arms and lowered his head for a long, slow kiss that turned my insides to mush.

"Mmm," I whispered into his lips when I finally caught my breath again, looking up into his dark gaze. "Alex ... this is insanely fast, you realize ..."

"I do realize." His thumb brushed the curve of my jaw lightly, touching me with tendrils of heat. "But what would be even more insane is not acknowledging that there's something between us, Chloe."

"Uh, yeah," I acknowledged incoherently when he kissed me again. "Okay, yeah. Mmm hmm ... this is so not good," I finally sighed, sinking into his tight embrace.

Alex drew back with a frown. "Why not?"

"Oh ... probably a lot of reasons. But the first one is that I'm already losing my mind and pregnancy brain hasn't even started yet."

He flashed a fast, wide grin that did illegal things to my heart rate. "I want to see you with pregnancy brain," he said simply, tucking my hand in his and guiding me into the best burger joint in the county.

He didn't let go even as the waiter guided us to a booth. Nope. We sat down and Alex was still clasping my hand in his, so I went ahead and gave him my other one, even as the waiter took our orders. "Are we gonna share a spaghetti plate?" I inquired.

"Better believe it. My middle name's Tramp." He winked and whatever part of my heart wasn't already his fell hard and fast.

"You remember *Lady and the Tramp*?" I demanded. "Nobody remembers that movie! Especially not guys!"

Alex shrugged one broad shoulder. "Like I keep telling you. There's something between us, Chloe. And if you think I'm going to let that slip away, you're dead wrong, sweets."

"I'm liking these endearments," I decided, pressing my palms to his and admiring how much larger his hands were than mine.

"I like you," he said softly, pressing my hand to his cheek. "Tell me the truth. Am I moving way too fast?"

I laughed. "Yes. Completely." As his face fell, I hastily added, "But I like it, Alex. I'm not a take-it-slow kind of girl. Never have been. You're right. It's really, really good between us. We just have a few issues that are kind of, well, between us."

He raised an eyebrow, clearly waiting for an explanation, but I waved a menu at him. "Can we pick first? I'm starving. *Someone* gave me a workout this morning ..."

With a smirk, he allowed me to peruse the menu and we

even managed to place orders for mega-size burgers, his rare, mine medium, his fries curly, mine sweet potato, before we returned to the topic at hand.

"Sweet potato fries?" He shook his head sadly. "I'm disappointed, Chloe."

"Only because you've never had them here," I retorted. "Try kissing me after I've had a bite of that cinnamon, sugary goodness and tell me you don't love them."

"Challenge accepted," he promised. "So ... things between us? Besides your appalling choice in sides?"

Some of my giddiness faded and I fidgeted with my napkin. "Well ... you know ..." I gestured vaguely at my midsection. "That's one thing. You're saying you're all in, Alex, but I'm not going to look like this much longer." I held up a hand before he could cut in again. "Far more importantly, in nine months it's not going to be just me. You're not the baby's father. It's not fair to ask you to stick around for parenthood, not before you even known enough to decide whether that's something you might eventually be interested in."

He was silent for so long after that that my heart sank and I finally muttered, "Well? You could say something. Anything."

"I was waiting to see if you were finished, since I kept interrupting you. Are you done?"

At least somewhat relieved, I nodded. "Yeah. Yeah. Please. Talk ..."

8

CHAPTER EIGHT

The look of uncertainty on her beautiful face made my gut twist. I nudged aside the sodas so I could lean in closer, recapturing her hands in mine. "Chloe," I said gently. "Look at me, honey."

Slowly, her face tilted back towards mine, finally meeting my gaze for the first time since she'd gone off on the baby tangent.

"This isn't what I expected," I began, squeezing her fingers. "At all. Not gonna deny that. The woman of my dreams walking onto a Greyhound and demanding the seat beside me?"

She laughed a little, blushing prettily.

"But you did," I went on. "And yeah, the baby is an unexpected factor, but the bottom line is, he or she is part of you. And I'm crazy about you, Chloe. So one way or another, I'll learn to be a parent. I ... want to be a parent," I added, as the realization settled over me. "It never occurred to me to think about kids, but with you ... it's just totally natural. It fits," I said quietly, meaning it with everything in me. "It's like ... I don't even have to question it or wonder about it. You fit perfectly in my life, Chloe and so does—"

"Alex!"

Both our heads jerked toward the sound of my shouted name. My eyes widened as David jogged straight into Malarky's, a place I was sure he'd never set in before in his life, and made a beeline for our booth.

"David, what—"

"Dad went into the hospital 40 minutes ago. I've been calling your phone for an age!"

THE RIDE to the hospital was a blur. David didn't bother to tell me how he'd tracked me down. Chloe and I crammed into his stupid-small sports car, so tiny that she was practically in my lap, and we sped across town, somehow avoiding the usual traffic cops.

Then we were on the small hospital's doorstep and I was sprinting toward the ER. Probably David and Chloe were following, but I was solely focused on Dad. It shocked me how concerned I was, when my dad and I had no relationship whatsoever. But I guess your father's your father, no matter what.

"Leonard Reed," I told the charge nurse. "He was just brought in?"

With a hospital this small and a family as notorious as mine, there was never any question about Dad's identity. The nurse nodded immediately, without even checking her records.

"This way." She led me down a yellow hallway, nowhere near as bleak as the walls that framed my usual workplace, and pulled back a curtain. To my immediate surprise, I spotted my father sitting up in bed, shirt off, his chest covered in electrodes, haranguing an intern.

Seeing me, he broke off and cursed in apparent relief. "Alexander. *Finally*. Will you tell this idiot that I require a full ..." he waved his hand uncertainly. "Whatever it is you call it."

"Workup," the intern supplied, looking like he was trying not to roll his eyes. I was familiar with the feeling when it came to Dad. "I've been trying to explain to Mr. and Mrs. Reed—"

"Your mother is so distraught that she's had one of her episodes," Dad informed me.

"Mrs. Reed is being attended to," the intern went on wearily. "As I was saying, we've ordered every recommended test..."

While he talked, I took the clipboard from him and half listened while studying the various studies they'd ordered, along with the notes on my father's condition when he was brought in.

"They want me dead," Dad howled with rage, as the intern wrapped up his narrative. "This town has been waiting for me to keel over for decades, in hopes of getting its hands on my money. Well, I'll have you know—"

"You're not dying, Dad," I said dryly. "What it looks like you may have is some heartburn, courtesy of your shitty diet and total lack of exercise. They're doing all the necessary tests to rule out any dangers, but those tests don't happen in five minutes. I'm sure they've told you that you'll be kept overnight."

"I should be here for a week," he snapped. "Heartburn! I knew that doctor training was an utter waste of my money."

"It wasn't your money," I reminded him. "I got a full ride. Now, if you'll excuse me, I should check on Mom ..."

I stepped past David and wondered briefly where Chloe had vanished to, but my whole focus was momentarily on dealing with my family's madness. She would understand, I was sure. That was the kind of person I already knew she was.

It wasn't hard to find Mom. I could hear her histrionics halfway down the hall and just followed them until I walked into the room where she was hyperventilating, waving off every attempt by medical staff to calm her.

"Don't give me sedatives! I'll die in my sleep!"

It would be a miracle if the hospital didn't poison both my parents' IVs before the night was through. Shooting an apologetic look at the doctor who was just exiting the room, I joined my mother at her bedside.

"Hi, Mom."

"Alex!" She grabbed my hand and dragged me close with a grip that no dying woman would ever be able to approximate. "This is my son. He's a *doctor*. He'll know how to care for me properly!"

"I don't have the slightest idea how to do that," I said bluntly, worn out by the sheer insanity that was my family. "Mom, you know you get these spells. You work yourself up and then they subside just as quickly as they begin."

Indeed, the 'spells' dated back to the earliest days of my childhood. Whenever Mom was unhappy with my clothes, my choice of food, my grades, my date, even my athletic abilities, a swoon would conveniently occur.

"I need my medicine," she said peremptorily, referring to some stupid vitamin or other that she'd started taking a decade back and was convinced held the cure to every ailment.

"You can't bring outside medications into a hospital, Mom. If you need medicine, they'll figure out exactly what and provide it."

That set her off on a wild rant and all I could do was sink into a chair, lock eyes with a sympathetic nurse, and wait for it to end.

CHAPTER NINE

Chloe

I jumped to my feet as David walked into the lobby, sipping distastefully at a cup of coffee. "Honestly, this has to be hot water and food dye."

"How is he?" I asked urgently.

The hospital staff had headed me off at the pass when David had informed them that I wasn't family. I'd been sitting waiting for what felt like forever, praying for some kind of good news.

"*They,*" David replied, trying another sip and making an identical grimace to the one he'd walked in wearing, "are fine."

"They?" I repeated uncertainly.

"Mother and Father," he clarified, tossing the full cup into a trashcan. "Come on. I need something with actual caffeine."

"What about Alex?" I asked. "And I thought it was just your father?"

"Alex is dealing with Mother," David replied, taking my arm and steering me toward the exit. "He'll be in there for a good while, so there's no point cooling our heels here."

Bewildered, I allowed myself to be led outside, where David stopped and considered various restaurant options in the vicinity before apparently deciding on one and starting across the street, half-dragging me.

"What happened to your mother?" I asked.

He rolled his eyes. "Father was having a cup of coffee—a *good* cup of coffee, I might add—during a business meeting. He's always had acid reflux but refuses to do anything Alex or the doctors tell him."

I noticed immediately that he didn't class his brother as a doctor and wondered why, but decided now was not the time to ask. We stopped at a crosswalk and waited for traffic to slow.

"He also had a massive breakfast full of everything he's not supposed to eat. So, in the middle of his meeting, he started feeling this heavy ache in his chest." My arm clasped firmly in his, David guided me across the street toward Java Joe's. "If you're not aware, my family has a tendency toward melodrama. He panicked and that probably worsened the heartburn. He collapsed on the floor and Mother was right there with him, shrieking hysterically and screaming for her own doctor."

I blinked, trying to take all that in as we walked up to the take-out only coffee joint. While David ordered, not bothering to ask if I wanted anything, I felt a deep sadness well up inside of me for Alex. My family had been far from perfect, but the chaos David had just described was nothing I'd ever experienced, not even on our worst days.

"Much better." He smacked his lips around what looked like a cappuccino and finally actually looked at me. "So. You're into Alex."

Stepping up to the window to order something to ward off the cold, I studiously avoided his gaze. It was so unlike his brother's. So cold. So … judging?

"Oh, sorry. Here. I've got it. What do you want?" David elbowed me aside and shoved a wad of cash at the cashier without even asking the price.

"Uh ... hot chocolate," I muttered.

"Not a fan of coffee?" he asked archly.

Why I told him, I don't know, but I did. "Caffeine isn't good for babies."

David's eyes went wide for just a second before his usual narrow-eyed gaze reasserted itself. "Aha," he said thoughtfully, as the cashier handed over my hot chocolate.

I cupped my hands around it, cold in more ways than one. "Aha?" I repeated.

"That explains your interest in my brother."

If I'd been taking a sip right then, I'd have spat it out all over myself. Thankfully, I'd barely lowered my nose for a sniff. "Excuse me?"

David smirked. "Don't playact with me, Chloe. My family is *very* familiar with your type."

"My type," I repeated, strangely numb in the face of what was very definitely some kind of insult. Usually I'd have let him have it with both guns blazing, but this was part of the issue I hadn't had a chance to discuss earlier with Alex ...

"Hangers on," he elaborated. "People in need of our class. And our cash."

Behind us, the cashier coughed violently and David swung around, probably to give him an earful. I took my chance and started away at a fast pace, but not fast enough. A moment later, he was beside me once more.

"Don't take it like that. We have. You don't. It's natural for you to want it."

"How is Alex even from your same family?" I muttered through clenched teeth.

"Oh, Alex is no saint," he promised me, and I could see his perfect grin from out of the corner of my eye, leering at me. "You do realize that you're just a project for him."

Now I stopped and turned to face David head on, my temper

finally flaring. "*Excuse* me?" Somehow it was one thing for him to tear into me, but for him to start in on his brother—

He laughed. "Look at you. Already thinking you're in love with him. Worse yet. Probably already thinking he's in love with you. Let me save you the heartache, sweetheart. The Reeds don't love commoners. Alex went to medical school to save the world, not to marry it. You're one of his little projects where he feels like he can redeem himself somehow by pulling you up out of the gutter."

The problem was that Paul's walking out on me had cut more deeply than I'd let on to anybody. I'd thought he was so into me ... and then he wasn't. So there was a chance that I might be making the same mistake again with Alex. Right?

"Poor Chloe," David droned on. "Let me take you home, sweets. It'll save you all kinds of heartache. Stress can't be any better for the baby than caffeine, right?"

I wanted to douse him in steaming hot chocolate. I really did. I was so close ...

"If you don't believe me, here's the evidence." Before I knew it, he'd shoved his phone under my nose. It was a conversation between him and Alex and much as I wanted to tear my eyes away, I was paralyzed.

Esme's hot, right? I'm not slumming?
She's gorgeous. And you're an ass.
Really? I'm not too good for her?
Man, she is way too good for you. When did you mutate, Dave?
So you don't see Chloe as slumming?
Unlike your feelings toward Esme, I'm too good for her.
Told you ...

Honestly, the conversation didn't even make sense. Something was seriously off. But all my brain saw was *I'm too good for her I'm too good for her I'm too good for her I'm too good for her.*

David patted my back sympathetically and I didn't even have

the strength to pull away. My mind was whirling with feelings of betrayal, warring with the belief that Alex was better than this. I knew he was.

Except. I didn't. That'd been the whole thing earlier, when he'd halfway told me he loved me and wanted to raise my baby with me—

My eyes filled with tears.

—and I'd tried to remind him that we barely knew each other.

"Right this way," David said quietly, and I stumbled along beside him in a daze. Somehow, I found myself in his car and somehow I then found myself back on my grandmother's doorstep, with David waving to me as he pulled away. "You're making the right decision, Chloe," he called. "For you and your baby. Alex has no part to play in your lives."

10
CHAPTER TEN

lex

A I should've walked out on Mom. And after I finally did, I should've walked out of the hospital, rather than going back to check on Dad. I had no connection with them whatsoever. I'd spent most of my life with them and yet I knew Chloe better than either one. But they were my parents and I wanted to help, even though several decades should have told me I couldn't.

By the time I finally walked into the lobby, bone weary and having accomplished nothing more than making my parents a) angrier and b) even more certain that my degree was a sham, all I wanted was to find Chloe and hold her close to me. No talking. Not even necessarily any kissing. I just wanted to be with her quietly, and I knew she'd understand exactly that need. Chloe understood everything.

Except, Chloe wasn't in the waiting room. And she didn't answer my call, or my texts.

"You were here for hours," David pointed out as he strolled into the waiting room with a fresh cup of coffee. "If you're looking for your girl, I'm guessing she split."

"No," I said firmly. "Chloe wouldn't just walk like that."

He snorted and handed me the coffee. "Here. Drink that. Maybe it'll thaw your brain. You don't know the girl, Alex."

I gave him a look even as I gratefully sipped the coffee. "Since when do you do nice things like remembering other people might need caffeine?"

"I'm a nicer guy than you think," he shrugged. "Look. It was like five hours you were in there. No girl who isn't married to you or seriously dating is going to wait around that long."

"Chloe's different," I insisted.

"And you say I'm selfish?" David said archly. "Dude. Pregnant lady? Exhausted, maybe?"

"How do you know she's pregnant?" I said in surprise, feeling guilt creep in at the truth of his words.

"She told me," he replied. "Right before she hit on me."

My free hand clenched into a fist. "Bullshit. Don't even go there, David. I mean it."

He rolled his eyes. "Why? Because you don't believe that your busgirl might just have a thing for the Reeds, rather than you?"

"*She's not like that.*"

"They're all like that, big bro. You'd think Chicago would have cleared up some of your chronic case of naivete. The girl acted all heartbroken for a little while and then she was suddenly all over me."

I lunged for David, splashing searing coffee everywhere and biting back a scream of pain and fury.

He danced back, his face grim. "Think about it. How else would I know about her pregnancy, Alex? She's desperate for someone to raise the kid. Someone with money."

The remains of my coffee splashed all over his shirt and my left hook collided powerfully with his right temple. Then I was out of the hospital, driving away from the Reed family drama as fast as I could.

I didn't believe a damn word out of David's mouth. Sure, I didn't know why he knew about her pregnancy, but I trusted Chloe. I hadn't realized up until that moment how much I trusted her above anyone else in my life. It was irrational and borderline insane, but hey, insanity clearly ran in my family.

Following that insanity, I took a sharp detour, ran a fast errand, and then jumped back in the car and hooked it toward Chloe's. She had to be there, waiting to find out how my parents were. True, I couldn't figure out why she wasn't answering my calls, but she'd have a good reason.

Pulling up in Chloe's driveway, I jumped out and was halfway to the door when her sister—the short, soft one—walked outside, arms folded across her chest. I slowed and waved tentatively, unsure what had changed the expression on her previously friendly face.

"Hi. Is, uh, Chloe in?"

"No," she said flatly, then didn't contribute further information.

"Um." I scratched the back of my neck, uncertain. "I'm not sure if she told you what happened—"

"She told us. You have some nerve showing up here. If Mara were around, you'd have a rifle stuck halfway up your behind."

I blinked in shock. "Wait. What? You don't understand."

"I understand plenty," she said tersely, every line in her face so rigid that it was obvious she was fighting back rage. "You've known my sister for all of a few days and yet somehow you still managed to wipe the floor with her heart worse than when the father of her baby walked out on her."

"I did what?" I exclaimed in shock. "Wait a minute. Look. My parents were both taken to the hospital. Chloe went with me and I guess they didn't let her because she wasn't family, so I kept her waiting for hours, I know. I'm really sorry. But they were my parents—"

"And she's my sister," the woman—Shannon, I finally remembered—cut in coolly. "She showed us the text. So you can quit your crap."

"Text?" I echoed. "What text? She didn't answer any of my texts!"

As I spoke, the Mercedes pulled up suddenly in the driveway, peeling in so hard that it kicked up a cloud of dust. Out of the Mercedes climbed tall and sharp Mara, her eyes blazing as she headed straight for me.

"You better run, boy."

Exasperated, I threw up my hands. "What the almighty fuck? All I want to know is where Chloe is!"

"Don't you presume to curse at me on my own land!" Mara snarled, walking up and poking me hard in the chest with nails like talons. "Not after you left my baby sister close to a zombie. When I loaded her on that bus, she was so lifeless I worried for her baby."

"*Bus?*" Tired of echoing everyone's words, I finally spat out my question. "Look. I have no idea what the fuhh—crap is going on here, other than that Chloe isn't here. For some reason you all think I've hurt her. But I would never do that. See?" Reaching into my pocket, I pulled out the small jeweler's box and popped the lid so they got an eyeful of the simple but brilliant ring. "It's not super fancy because I didn't think she'd be into that. But it sparkles. Like, uh, her eyes. So why would I get her this if I didn't love her? If I didn't want to commit to her?"

Both Mara and Shannon had actually gone silent for a few minutes. When Shannon finally spoke, her tone had thawed very slightly.

"You don't even know her."

"I know her enough to love her. And you're telling me that she's on a bus? Headed where?" I asked desperately. "And why, for God's sake?"

The look the two women exchanged between them sent chills down my spine before Mara finally said, "You better come in."

CHAPTER ELEVEN

Chloe

The bus was louder than the one I'd taken earlier in the week, what seemed like a full century back. Having left my phone at the house and practically everything else, I had nothing to block the sound. So I wrapped my head in my sweater and tried to sink into some kind of coma where there was no sound and no pain. No vision of Alex dancing in front of my eyes, typing out those cruel words.

Too numb to even cry, I rested my palm over my unborn child and whispered, "Just you and me, little one. Somehow, we'll make it work. Just like we were planning before he walked into our lives."

Technically, I'd walked into his, I had to admit. I'd forced myself into the seat beside his and now I was paying dearly for my temerity.

I didn't ask to love him, I whispered to myself. *That was never part of the plan.*

But I had, almost immediately. Something about that stupid newspaper, his immediate surly attitude, followed by the shift to total protectiveness, had reeled me in like a fish. And now I was left flopping on the line, struggling to breathe.

God, what a morbid image, but it was exactly how I felt. He'd played me for a total fool, gotten me in bed almost instantly, and then laughed about it behind my back, undoubtedly just waiting for me to head back to Chicago at which point I'd never hear from him again.

The air beneath the hoodie was getting stuffy, so I finally shoved it back and took a deep breath in. The noise was still there. Screaming baby in the back; arguing couple on my left; someone's non-soundproof earbuds in the near vicinity, venting misogynistic lyrics every which way.

"You okay?" my seatmate asked sympathetically.

He was a gray-haired guy, actually someone I could see reading a paper. His face was creased and kind, almost making me tear up. But not quite. I couldn't let go until I got back home. Then I'd wallow for a few days before picking myself up and moving on with my life.

"I'm ... fine," I mumbled, reaching for the water bottle Mara had insisted I take, if nothing else.

"You've been tossing and turning for over an hour." He shook his head. "Doesn't seem fine to me."

"Has it been that long already?" I scrubbed at my eyes in disbelief. "Sorry, have I kept you awake?"

"You're fine," he assured me. "I rarely sleep in automobiles. Leaves me queasy."

Nodding, trying to remain polite while utterly uninterested in conversation with anyone, I squeezed past him and stumbled down the aisle to the bathroom. Predictably, it was less than clean but at least I managed to wash my face and even attempt to square my shoulders in the mirror, giving myself a stern lecture.

"You didn't know him. Whatever you're feeling is an exaggeration, probably because of your pregnancy hormones. You may have thought you loved him, but you didn't. And even if you did, he was way out of your social stratosphere. There was never any chance, kid. Just deal with it."

Shaking my head and trying to force myself to believe, I stepped out of the bathroom and discovered to my surprise that we were stopped. With relief and more than a little confusion, I stood in the back and watched everyone in the bus, screaming baby included, vacate the premises.

The driver glanced at the way I was protectively holding my stomach, something that was becoming more instinctive by the minute, and nodded. "You can stay on the bus, miss. We're having some mechanical trouble and just sent for another bus to come meet us so you all can transfer onto it. Go ahead and get you some rest while it's quiet."

Gratefully, I sank down into my seat, minus my chatty seatmate, and reached for my hoodie once more.

Time must have passed. I wasn't sure how long, but I actually managed to doze a little, until my seatmate returned and gripped my shoulder, shaking me, clearly telling me to move out of his window seat. It was just so much easier to rest when my head was pillowed on the glass, rather than my own shoulder, though.

"Chloe. Chloe. Damn it, Chloe, wake up."

I frowned and blinked away the sleep, wondering how my seatmate knew my name. "Leave me alone. Just a little more sleep, please, then we can switch seats."

"Chloe!"

The abrupt change in volume had me shooting upright. I shoved the hoodie away in alarm and suddenly everything swam into focus.

Alex stood in the aisle, his jaw set grimly.

"No. You're not here," I muttered. "I'm on a bus, headed

home."

"Honey, your bus left a good while back," he replied, with a note in his voice that I couldn't decipher.

"What are you talking about? We were going to transfer—"

"And they all did. You slept through it. And now you're awake and you and I are going to talk."

"What?" I said in horror, scrambling to my feet and almost smacking my head on the overhead baggage rack. "No. I need to be on that bus!"

"No. You need to be with me." Alex blocked my exit from the seat, his big body preventing me from any chance of a sneak getaway. "You hurt me, Chloe."

"*I* hurt you?" I said in amazement. "Please. I saw the texts, Alex. I know you played me."

"I thought we knew each other," he said quietly. "In spite of only, you know, *knowing* each other a few days. I really thought we got one another."

"So did I," I blurted out, tears rising to my eyes and starting to slip down my cheeks in spite of my earlier resolution.

"Honey, I didn't write that message. Or rather, I did, but not the way you think." Pulling out his phone, Alex pushed it into my hands and then stood there, waiting.

"I don't want to read it again," I whispered.

"Please, Chloe. Give me a chance. Just one chance?"

The pleading in his tone broke me and with extreme reluctance, my eyes so blurred I could barely make out the screen, I glanced at the words I'd memorized.

Esme's hot, right? I'm not slumming?

She's gorgeous. And you're an ass.

Really? I'm not too good for her?

Man, she is way too good for you, I texted back wearily. *When did you mutate, Dave?*

So you don't see Chloe as slumming?

Unlike your feelings toward Esme, I'm too good for her.
Told you ...

That's not what I meant! I'm not too good for her. Chloe is amazing. And if Esme is as smart as I remember her being, she'll run screaming from you.

Esme's mean. I like em that way.

I read and re-read the words, tears still dripping down my cheeks, before the penny finally dropped. "Oh." Dismayed now in a totally different way, I looked up at Alex where he still stood, his expression totally blank. "Oh ... Alex ..."

"You should've trusted me," he said gruffly. "It kills me that you didn't. It makes me want to throw in the towel just like you tried to, because I believed that you, of all people, believed in me."

"I do believe in you!" I blurted. "Oh my God. Alex, please—"

"My entire family thinks I'm a failure and essentially a washed up nothing. The people who are supposed to know me best think I'm gutter trash. I believed that you knew me better, Chloe."

The sad look in his eyes killed me, but he kept talking.

"But you know what? Of course you didn't know. Because the truth is what you kept trying to tell me at Malarky's. We don't know each other. Not deeply, anyway, however much we connect."

I covered my mouth with my hand, outright sobbing now. "Alex. I'm sorry. I'm so sorry."

"It's okay," he said so quietly that I almost didn't hear him.

I raised my head from my chest and stared at him through reddened eyes. "Huh?"

"I said it's okay, Chloe. Because you may not know me very well yet, but I plan on spending the rest of my life helping you get to know me."

As he spoke, he got down on one knee in the tiny aisle and

held out his palm. On it sat a box. A box with a ring. A brilliant, sparkling, movie star ring that made my mouth go dry, even as I cried harder still.

"I love you, Chloe." He looked up at me, his eyes so warm and tender that if I hadn't already been a red, sniffly mess, he would've reduced me to one. "This isn't a Marry Me. I know it's way too early for that. This is a Get to Know Me. You can say yes to me later on down the line. But just know that Yes is the ultimate goal. I love you, and I love your baby. And that is never going to change. Please, Chloe. Will you get to know me?"

It was way too early, yes, but that didn't make one bit of difference as I also knelt awkwardly, wrapped my arms around Alex, and kissed him over and over again, my tears promptly soaking him.

"I love you too," I told him over and over again, framing his face with my hands. "I love you so much it's ridiculous. And I'm sorry I didn't trust you. Forgive me?"

"I forgave you for stealing my seat that first day," he teased, kissing my nose and eyes and cheeks before finally, tenderly, drawing me into the sweetest kiss. "I'll forgive you for anything, Chloe. Just get to know me. And let me get to know you, in every single way."

"Yes." I held him close to me and whispered the words into his lips, laughing and crying at the same time as he slid the gorgeous Get to Know Me ring on my finger. "Yes. Yes. Yes."

THE END

SIGN UP TO RECEIVE FREE BOOKS

Sign Up to Receive Free E-Books and Audiobook Codes.

WOULD you like to read **The Unexpected Nanny, Dirty Little Virgin** and **other romance books for free?**

YOU CAN SIGN up to receive these free e-books and audiobooks by typing this link into your browser:

HTTPS://WWW.STEAMYROMANCE.INFO/FREE-BOOKS-AND-AUDIOBOOKS-HOT-AND-STEAMY/

OR THIS ONE:

. . .

HTTPS://WWW.STEAMYROMANCE.INFO/THE-UNEXPECTED-NANNY-FREE/

PREVIEW OF DESTINED DESIRES
A BAD BOY BILLIONAIRE ROMANCE

By Alizeh Valentine

Blurb

What can I say about Cade Lowell?
I can say that he's arrogant, domineering, and is used to having things his own way.
I would also have to say that he's hot as hell and that absolutely nothing has changed since we broke up in high school—he leaves me just as breathless and frustrated as he did back then, when he was the only one who had ever touched me.
He was just a boy the last time I saw him, but when I return to White Pines to deal with my late grandmother's house, I realize that he's all man now!
I feel electric when I'm around him, and I can tell right away he wants me too, but there's more to love than heat.
Will he ever get past his arrogant ways to see that I want a say in things too?

The Doctor's Claim

When Mara's car ends up in a ditch on a snowy night, who should rescue her but Cade Lowell, her high school sweetheart? Sparks start flying, but can they make it work this time?

Cade thought he was over the idea of love and family, but a chance encounter with Mara, the one who got away, makes him wonder if he can see a future in her green eyes.

Mara's past comes calling in the form of her high school boyfriend, Cade, who's all grown up, rich, and hotter than hell. Can they leave the past behind and find a Christmas romance?

CHAPTER ONE

Mara

It was technically still daylight when I left my youngest sister's house in Illinois. She had said goodbye to me, but Chloe hadn't been able to take her eyes away from Alex Reed, who had been standing there all apologetic, desperate to make amends.

They really are cute together, I thought with some amusement. Even if Alex was closer to my age than my sister's, I couldn't help regarding them both with a big sister's eye. *Really, all that trouble over a little romance.*

Despite my amusement, I was happy for my fey little Chloe. Alex would steady her, and she would maybe help him take that stick out of his well-bred, rich-boy ass. He had been nearly silent all through our drive from White Pines to Elgin, so grim-faced and determined to make things up to Chloe that I thought he might pop a vein. All he had wanted was Chloe's address so that he could drive to see her, but I had refused. No way, no how.

Nope, not if she doesn't know you're coming and might be unhappy to see you. I'll drive, or you're not getting a thing from me.

Alex Reed has at least one brother, so he should know what it's like to be simultaneously frustrated with someone and incredibly protective of them. Now here I am, leaving my sister to her happy ending and making the drive north to White Pines again.

Shannon, the middle of us Becker sisters, was probably going to be waiting up for me, and I winced a little at the thought. We still needed to talk about what we were going to do with our grandmother's house, and that wasn't a conversation either of us was looking forward to. Chloe had said she would go along with whatever Shannon and I decided, and I barely avoided rolling my eyes. Of course Chloe weaseled her way out of the difficult decisions and went home with a rich, handsome doctor. Par for the course for Chloe.

I had been hoping to get back to White Pine by eight or nine, but as the sky darkened and large clumpy snowflakes started to fall, I pushed that estimation back, and then pushed it back again. My car, a powerful and elderly Mercedes, drove just fine in the cold and snow, but the snow was coming faster and faster. I saw other cars peeling off the exits, the traffic thinning out, but I kept going.

It'll be fine. I'll just take it slow...

That mantra actually worked at convincing me for almost four hours of white-knuckled driving. I drove slowly but steadily, staring so hard into the swirling white blankness ahead of me that I felt as if my eyes were drying out. Time took on a peculiarly elastic quality. I felt as if I had been on the road forever. It felt as if I would never get to White Pines. Then, miracle of miracles, I saw a sign saying I was just twenty miles away from the city limits.

"Oh thank god," I muttered.

Afterward, I couldn't figure out if it was the release of that vital bit of tension that caused what happened next, or if it was just some strange twist of fate. I was focused on the road, the conditions actually looking as if they were clearing up, and then there was a deer standing stock still in the middle of the road.

As it was happening, it felt as if time stood still. It felt as if I had all the time in the world to look at the deer; to take in its dark eyes, its spindly legs, the round barrel of its body. All of this I saw as I wrenched the wheel to the side with a cry of shock. The deer seemed to wait until the last minute to run out of the way, and when I saw that I had cleared it, I tried to yank the car back onto the road.

With a sense of inevitability, I felt the tires spinning underneath me as the car fishtailed, sliding backwards straight into the ditch. I rocked hard against my seat belt, and for a moment, everything went dark.

THE NEXT THING I KNEW, there was a frantic tapping on the window, and I could see red lights flashing some small distance away.

Oh god, is it the cops?

I hastened to roll down the window an inch. Now I could see the man in the dark wool coat on the other side, a scarf pulled up to protect his face and a knit cap pulled down over his ears.

"Are you all right?" he asked. "I saw your car in the ditch."

My first instinct was to say that of course I was all right, but instead, I took a moment to assess myself. I was definitely bruised and sore, but there was nothing overtly wrong with me. There was no tenderness at all around my head; I had likely simply blacked out from surprise, not impact.

"I think I'm all right," I said, and the man nodded.

"Good. Turn off your car. I'll help you get to mine."

I turned off the engine, and I couldn't help feeling as if I had just pulled the plug on my beloved old car's life support. The thought made me feel oddly queasy, but I shoved it away, looking instead at the man on the other side of the door.

"Are you a cop?" I asked.

"Sorry, no," he said. "But come on, I'll take you up the road to White Pines, at least."

I debated with myself for a minute, and then shrugged. The wind was howling, the car, now that it was off, was cooling off quickly, and I didn't relish waiting for a cop to finally show up.

"All right, just...please don't be a serial killer or anything, all right?"

He laughed at that, and I was surprised by how much I enjoyed the sound of his laughter. When I opened the door, he steadied me in the frozen weeds by the side of the road. I looked at my car, which looked like a wounded animal in the ditch, and sighed. But there was nothing to be done about that now. I followed him back to his car with its hazards blinking on the side of the road, and before I got in, I whipped out my phone and took a picture of his license plate defiantly.

"What's that all about?" my rescuer asked as he got into the car. To my relief, the heat had been left running, and I focused on forcing some life back to my fingertips. Even that short amount of time outside had left them a little numb.

"Texting it to my sister, to make sure that you actually get me to White Pines," I said, flashing him a wide grin. My cocky attitude dared him to have a problem with my precaution. How a man reacted when a woman did something as simple as ensure her own safety was always telling. Some men understood, others got angry. This one laughed.

"Well, you haven't changed a bit, have you, Mara?" he asked. "Still the same suspicious girl with the bright green eyes."

I felt a chill run up my spine as all sorts of explanations for his words tumbled through my mind. My hand was on the door handle when he put the car in drive and pulled away from the edge of the road. If he had moved one moment slower, I might have jumped into the blizzard and taken my chances.

"Who the hell are you?" I demanded, feeling a little defensive—of course I was suspicious. When had the world ever given me a reason not to be?

"You're going to hurt my feelings, darling," he drawled. The car was warming up, and he pulled off the knit cap to reveal a head of thick, dark hair. When he glanced at me, a dozen half-intuited hints fell into place before my brain could fully catch up with what I was seeing. His face was leaner than it had been at eighteen. The strong bones there were starker, but the dark hair was the same, as were the gray eyes, visible in the overhead light.

My hand flew to my mouth, covering it in surprise.

"Cade..." I murmured. My tongue stuttered over his name, but the rest of me remembered well enough. It felt as if a forest fire raced through my body, making me draw a sharp breath.

"Good to see you too, darling," Cade said sardonically, a twinkle in his eyes, and we drove toward White Pines.

CHAPTER TWO

Cade

I had never been one to believe in fate, and I wasn't sure that I did right then. I certainly hadn't been thinking of fate when I saw the car in front of me spin off the road; the winking white tail of a deer disappearing on the other side of the road. Instead, my mind had been filled with images of death and blood, and when the woman in the car had finally stirred, I had felt a relief so profound it made me weak in the knees.

After that, all I could think about was getting her to safety and making sure she was well. I had actually liked it when she took the picture of my license plate. There was something about the sharp way she answered me, her take-no-prisoners attitude, that drew me to her like a magnet. That was when I'd recognized her. I'd recognized the sharpness of her voice, the defiant lift of her chin, and of course by those green, green eyes that could take a man apart.

It was Mara.

It was Mara fucking Becker that I had pulled out of the snow, and if that wasn't fate, it was at least proof that the universe had a sense of humor.

"God, Cade," she said, and something in me thought I could hear some kind of warmth in her tone. If there was warmth there, I told myself not to trust it, but Mara had always been a straight shooter...about most things, anyway.

"What are you doing out here?"

"Oh the usual," I said. "Dashing around in the snow, rescuing pretty girls. Being my regular irresponsible self."

God, what the hell was wrong with me? I sounded like a snarky teenager, and she would have had every right to take my head off for it. Instead she laughed a little; a warm sound that made something inside me come undone.

"I'm not going to question it," she said with a light laugh. "I know for a fact that you would have stopped for me ten years ago. The fact that you were still willing to stop now...I think that's to your credit."

Praise from the queen herself. It took effort to stop myself from warming underneath her words. I had been down that path before, and I knew that it didn't lead anywhere good.

"Didn't do it for your approval, princess," I said with a shrug. "I would have stopped for anyone."

"Good," she said, a little tartness entering her tone as well. "Do you want a medal for not checking to see whether a girl is cute or not before you help her out of a wreck?"

I wanted to snap my teeth at her, and that was familiar too. Instead, I ignored her, choosing to focus on driving. The blizzard wasn't too bad, and the reports said that it would stop by two or three in the morning. My car could handle it, but I could end up in a ditch as easily as she had.

In the old days, Mara would have sailed into a fight with her banner held high, or she would have stalked off with way more dignity and verve than any teenage girl should have. Now, though, she simply looked at me through the darkness. I could feel her gaze on me like a touch, and I drew a deep breath into my lungs, letting it out slowly.

When I thought back to Mara and White Pines, I could never escape a shudder of pleasure; always hot, but as I grew older, strange as well. Christ, there had been plenty of women since Mara, the oldest of the Becker girls, but they were mostly gone and forgotten. None of them could draw a shudder from me the way the mere thought of Mara could. Now that she was in my passenger's seat, fully grown and with those same green eyes, those same full lips, I realized I hadn't been imagining it.

I still wanted her, and that thought pissed me off.

"What the hell are you looking at?" I asked, and she laughed again.

"You, of course," she said, and there was no anger in her voice at all. "Are you still so angry at me?"

"I'd have to be pretty insane to still be mad about something that happened ten years ago," I said gruffly. "Christ, we were kids."

"That didn't answer my question," Mara said, but she didn't press. She looked out her window at the sleeting blizzard, and when she spoke again, there was a slightly dreamy quality to her voice.

"I was mad at you for a long time, you know," she said. "I might not have had a reason to be, but I was. I thought...I thought you had ruined a perfectly good thing, but now maybe I see why you did it. Why you left. Maybe it was even good that you did."

That stung more than I thought it would. I could remember my last few nights in White Pines ten years ago. They weren't pleasant at all. The only person that had made them bearable was sitting beside me right now.

"Was I right?" I asked. I had meant for it to come out snidely, but it was a real question. "About what you did, I mean. Did you go to a nice college out east, marry some guy with a portfolio and a perfect credit score at twenty-two, and have an adorable kid by twenty-four?"

"I think you just described the first three or four guys I dated," she said with a little laugh. "But no to the rest. That type of guy tends to want a housekeeper and a nanny more than a partner, and when I figured that out, I dropped out and moved to Atlanta."

I couldn't stop myself from laughing at that, and she shot me a look that was slightly irritated.

"Miss Valedictorian dropped out?"

"As a matter of fact, I did," she retorted. "It was absolutely the right choice. I wasn't meant to work in business administration. I could see that I was surrounded by the kind of people I already wanted to kill at the age of nineteen, and if I'd kept on going with that crowd, I might have actually done it at twenty-five."

"All right," I said, conciliatory in spite of myself. "I'm sure that speech worked on your parents. What did you do instead? What was in Atlanta?"

"A guy," she admitted, so shamefaced that I laughed again. "God, I wasn't even twenty, but I thought he knew everything—it was just dumb. We lasted about ten minutes after I'd moved down there."

"But you didn't move back?"

"No. I had too much pride, but once I'd gotten over that, I'd fallen in love with the city, and by then I'd secured a magazine job. I'm an editor now. It's good work. I can do it on the road when I like. And it pays well enough."

I risked sneaking a look at her again. She wasn't looking at me, and she wasn't expecting me to be looking at her at all. There was a faint line of tension between her eyes.

"But it's not what you want to be doing."

She flashed me a sharp grin.

"What about you? Are you living your dream?" she asked. "Seeing the United States, odd jobs, the great American experience?"

That was familiar. God, I had been ridiculous at eighteen, but a part of me still bridled at her tone.

"You're not the only one who's changed, Mara," I retorted. "I bummed around the country for about two years. Crossed it half a dozen times, worked on a shrimping boat off the Gulf. Then my uncle called me up and told me he had some work for me. I'm in real estate now."

The way I said it, she would have been within her rights to guess that I worked for a landlord somewhere. When she laughed, I bristled, but when I felt her hand move over and touch mine on the wheel, something in me almost purred.

"I thought about you," she whispered, as if it were a confession. "And yes, you were on that damned bike of yours, roaring along the freeway, stopping in towns for a few weeks to get enough gas money to keep going. I can see you on the Gulf, too. I've been there a few times, where the water's so blue it takes your breath away and the sun rises out of it all red, looking like it's on fire...Were you happy then?"

"No," I said bluntly. "It was fun. I had some wild times, but it wasn't right."

"And what you're doing now?"

"Getting closer to right, maybe."

"I'm glad."

She sounded like she meant it, and I had to actually search for the anger I'd always kept right next to my need for her. God, the fact that she could disarm me in less than half an hour would be hilarious if it wasn't so pathetic. I stayed quiet the rest of the way to White Pines, and then I automatically drove her to her grandmother's house.

"Having a family vacation at your grandma's?" I asked as we pulled up.

"No, she's been dead for a few years," Mara said bluntly. Even as calm and steady as her voice was, there was a hurt there that made me want to take her in my arms. "The property got through probate, and now my sisters and I need to figure out what we're doing with it."

She wasn't as calm about all of this as she wanted me to think she was, or that she wanted to be herself, but it wasn't my place to press her. Instead, I got out of the car and went around to open her door for her, and she smiled at me, ever the princess.

"This is where I get off," she said needlessly, but she didn't walk up the stairs toward the door. "Maybe we'll see—"

I could lie and say that I couldn't help myself in that moment, that it was all the memories and need, and maybe just a small urge to rewrite the past. Tell the truth and shame the devil, though, it was only because I wanted her. In the dim porch light, with the snow whirling around us and getting caught in her dark hair, I wanted her—and so I pulled her to me and kissed her.

She tasted as good as I remembered, all warm and sweet, and after a moment of frozen shock, she pressed herself against me. We were both bundled up against the cold, but I could feel the warmth of her rising to meet me. I couldn't stop myself from burying my hands in her hair, holding her still so I could explore her mouth, learning her all over again, showing her how badly I wanted her...

Just as quickly as we had reached for each other, we pulled away again. We stared at each other, and I realized that I couldn't read her at all. We were adults now, not the crazy kids we had been before. There was an entire decade gaping between us, and despite what some part of me tried to insist, we didn't know each other anymore.

I started to say something, some apology, something to explain away what we had done, but then the door at the top of the stairs opened, spilling a harsh light over us.

"Oh my god, Mara? Are you all right? I've been calling you..."

Shannon, my brain helpfully supplied. Standing in pajamas and a robe at the top of the stairs, she stared at us wide-eyed and confused. There were really no explanations for either of us to make, so I turned to Mara.

"See you later," I murmured.

"Wait," she blurted out, but I was already getting back in the car, heading back toward my hotel on the other side of town. I tried to tell myself that I was in White Pines to do work, not to mess around with my high-school sweetheart; but as I drove through the swirling snow listening to the wind whistle through my windows, I knew that it was only the barest thread of self-control that kept me driving ahead instead of turning around and finding that warmth that I had only ever shared with Mara Becker.

CHAPTER THREE

Mara

"Was that...?"

"Cade Lowell, yes, it was," I said brusquely. "Come on, we need to get inside before the cold gets both of us."

Shannon followed me inside with a frown, and when I stripped out of my winter gear, I could finally breathe a sigh of relief. As I did so, I could smell something utterly amazing in the air, and I turned to Shannon with surprise.

"Did you bake a pie?"

"I did," she said with a slight smile. "And there's some stew as well. I was hoping to eat with you, but there's plenty leftover. You can eat and tell me what the hell happened with Chloe. And with Cade as well, apparently."

I wasn't used to having to answer to people any more, I realized, following her to the kitchen. I worked independently in Atlanta, and I could go days without needing to go into the magazine's office. Even as I noticed it, however, I also noticed how nice it was having my sister sit across from me in our grandmother's old house, ladling out a bowl of stew and cutting off a hunk of thick bread before laying them down in front of me.

"God, Shannon, did you bake bread too?"

"I was on my own all day," she said with a faint smile. "I had to do something, didn't I? Eat, and then talk."

We hadn't been at our best the past little while as we tried to figure out everything with the house. The food and her gentle bullying felt like something of a truce, and I was tired enough that I wanted to take it. The food was good enough that I couldn't even savor it, scarfing it down while putting off her expectant gaze.

Talking about Chloe and Alex was easy. Shannon nodded and agreed that it seemed like they were good for each other, but I didn't miss the wistful look in her eyes. My sister has always been a bit of a romantic, but romance always seemed to pass her by. I could have told her it wasn't really that great anyway, but that conversation never seemed to go all that well.

"So much for Chloe and Alex," she mused. "Now tell me what's going on with you and Cade. Have you guys, I don't know, gotten together again after all this time?"

I winced a little at her curiosity, because if I was honest, I didn't know what to make of it myself. Ever since Cade had picked me up, I felt as if everything in my head had been shaken up; thrown around as if in a hurricane. That shouldn't have surprised me, however. That was just Cade. He came in like a storm, and when he left, nothing was the same.

He had done it to me once before, after all.

T*en* Y*ears* A*go*

"Hey Mara, it's Cade again!"

Sammi, one of my classmates, drew out Cade's name like taffy, shrill and taunting, but underneath it, I could hear her envy clear as day. I shot her a dirty look and walked over to the window, refusing to let myself hurry.

I was acting as cool as I could, but the truth was I couldn't stop my heart from skipping a beat. I had transferred to White Pines to finish out my senior year because my grandma needed some help after a fall. I knew why my parents sent me, but I had figured it would be a dull and lonely time, far away from my family and my friends.

What I hadn't counted on was Cade Lowell, who had stopped me at Malarky's, paid for my burger and then insisted on eating with me. That was almost six weeks ago, and we'd been seeing each other every day since.

He was on that motorcycle of his that made Grandma fret every time he came to pick me up, and he was completely at ease on it. That was maybe my favorite thing about Cade: how easy he was about everything. He was dressed in black jeans, heavy boots, a black T-shirt and, of course, the omnipresent black motorcycle jacket. It was heavy enough to be armor, and that's how I always thought of it.

"What do you want?" I asked with a mock scowl. "Did Carson decide you were too much trouble and fire you or something?"

Cade grinned, unperturbed, open and easy.

"Turns out his kid is getting married tomorrow in Madison so he closed up the garage for the day. I'm heading up to the quarry. Come with me."

"You think I've got nothing better to do than to come with you?" I teased, and his grin turned a little more sly.

"I might make it worth your while," he offered.

I scoffed, but a pleasant warmth was already spreading in my belly, making me want to blush. I pretended to think about it for a minute, and then glanced over my shoulder where a half-dozen other students were fussing over layouts for the school yearbook. I was only there because I had some experience with graphic design, and I was already bored.

"All right, I'll be right down."

I got some glares as I walked out of the room, but it didn't matter. That bright spring afternoon, the only thing I cared about was Cade and getting as close to him as I could.

Cade gave me a helmet and made sure I was clinging tight to him before he roared down the road. Every time I got on his bike with him, I felt a deep thrill of danger and pleasure twine together inside me. When I pressed my cheek to his shoulder, I smelled leather and sweat. I never felt more grown up than I did with Cade.

The ride to the quarry was a short one, and soon enough, we had pulled over onto one of the small side roads that wormed their way all over the area. We left his bike in a sheltered spot and walked hand in hand up one of the narrow paths. He let me walk ahead of him, and I could feel his eyes on my rear and my hips. I knew that if I were at home, my parents would never let me go off alone with Cade. He was my age, and still attended high school for half the day, working the other half, but there was something more adult about him, more dangerous.

Cade and I found a tree with plenty of soft grass underneath, and we curled up on the ground below, my head pillowed on his shoulder.

"How are things at home?" I asked, and he shrugged.

"Dad somehow missed his usual weekend bender, so he's making up for it now. I might just sleep at the garage if he gets too bad."

I winced. Cade's father had a reputation in town, and it wasn't a pleasant one.

"You could come over to my place," I suggested. "There's a spare bedroom."

Cade laughed, shaking himself a little.

"Bet your grandma would love that," he said. "Nah, the garage is good. Its got a TV, some books. No big deal. But I don't want to talk about that right now."

"Oh?" I asked, amused. "What do you want to talk about?"

As it turned out, he didn't want to talk at all, and as way lay curled up under the tree overlooking the quarry, he started to kiss me. We moved against each other, kissing and learning and exploring until all I could hear was our breathing, the slide of our clothed bodies rubbing against each other, our heartbeats thudding as loudly as drums.

I wanted him more than I had wanted anything in my life, but when he started to unzip my jeans, I put my hand over his.

"No," I said. "I don't want that..."

Cade blew hair through his lips, pressing his forehead against my shoulder, and reluctantly nodded. He flopped over onto his back, one arm thrown over his eyes, and I appreciated the opportunity to recover myself.

"Such a good girl," he teased when we had both caught our breath a little bit.

Honestly, I didn't even know why I had stopped him. All I knew was that even if I wanted him something fierce, I didn't want him yet, and I was grateful that he seemed to understood.

After a while, we curled up next to each other again, kissing a little, talking more. I listened with half an ear as he talked about getting on his bike to see the country, going from town to town, learning all the ways people were alike and all the ways they were different. I was more worried about my grandma and how frail she seemed with every passing day.

When the sun started to inch toward the horizon, he took me back to town, dropping me off in front of my grandma's house.

"I'm going to be working on a project for the next few days, but maybe I could see you on Friday?"

"Sounds good," I said. "Sure you won't agree to scandalize the neighborhood and stay in our spare bedroom?"

He laughed.

"Nah. I'm good. See ya, princess."

Friday night came, and I ignored the school chatter about the upcoming spring dance. It all felt very far away to me: all of the talk of who was going, who wasn't. Instead I went home, checked with my grandma to make sure she had taken all of her medications, and went to read on the porch for a while.

Around dusk, just as I was getting ready to give up and go inside, I heard the thunder of Cade's motorcycle. I put my book down and rose up to meet him, a wide smile on my face. When he dismounted and wrapped his arms around me, I felt as light as a feather, like a bit of ash thrown up from a bonfire drifting back down to earth.

"Hi," I said softly. "What do you want to do tonight?"

He grinned at me.

"Want to go to Chicago?"

I blinked, laughing in half-disbelief.

"What, you mean like...for the weekend? Cade, you know I can't leave my grandma..."

"No, not for the weekend, maybe for like a week. There's a guy down there that needs all the hands he can get for some kind of production push, and then after that, I don't know. Maybe down to New Orleans. I've always wanted to see the Gulf. I think my mom's people were from there. Or Los Angeles. Why not?"

I stared at him, because despite the sheer insanity that was spilling out of his mouth, there was a part of me that wanted nothing more than to get on his bike with him. I had to push back from him because I was suddenly so tempted I couldn't stand it.

"What the hell are you talking about, Cade?" I hissed. "Are you leaving? What about...what about school? What about graduation?"

Cade's face hardened.

"If I want a diploma, I'll get a GED, but I don't want one. I don't want to stay one more minute in this damn town. I've been spending the last few days getting things together, getting some cash, packing up, and now all I need is for you to come with me."

The confusion that been bubbling up inside me swiftly turned to anger, and I glared at him.

"You mean that you decided to do this just a few days ago, and now you expect me to drop everything and come with you?"

The look he gave me was impatient. He reached for my hand, but I pulled away.

"Come on, Mara, you know you're too good for this town. You know that you want to come with me."

"I *know* that I'm graduating from this damn high school in a few months, and I *know* that I need to stay here and look after my grandmother," I snapped. "I thought you knew that, but apparently not."

He looked a little guilty at the mention of my grandmother, but he refused to back down.

"I want you with me," he said. "We would be awesome together on the road, you know that. I don't want to do this without you."

"But you will," I said sadly, reading the decision in his eyes. "Because you've decided, haven't you? I either come with you now with absolutely no preparation, no regard for my responsibilities, and no safety net if everything goes wrong, or it's over."

Cade looked stricken, but I refused to quit.

"God, Cade. You can't do this to me. You can't just make a decision and insist that I fall in line like some kind of doll!"

"That's not what I want," he growled. "You know that. I want us to get out of this damn town, and I want us to be ourselves. I want to be with you, and I don't want to be Daniel Lowell's son who's probably going to end up just like him if I don't get the hell out."

"You can't ask me to do this," I repeated, and to my dismay, he took a step back. When I reached for his hand, he shook me off.

"Fine," Cade said. "You want a life that you can predict down to the millimeter? You want to go to a nice college and marry a nice man and live out in the suburbs wondering where the hell your life went, fine."

He turned away, striding back toward his bike, and this time, I was the one who tried to hang on to his hand.

"Cade...don't..."

He glanced back at me, and his gray eyes were so angry that I fell back a pace. I suddenly remembered all of those people who had said that Cade Lowell had a temper, who had told me he could be violent and cruel, and for the first time I was afraid of him.

"You told me what you want, princess," he spat. "And that's fine. If that's the way you want to live your life, fantastic. That's not what I want for myself."

I was so stunned by his words that I was completely mute as he got on his motorcycle again. I watched as he gunned the bike down the street, and even though I knew most of the neighborhood was watching me, I stood on the drive and stared after him long after I was gone.

"You never told us about any of that," Shannon said quietly, eyes wide.

"Well, I stayed at Grandma's for most of that summer, and then I moved home for all of two weeks before I started college." I shrugged. "It didn't seem like there was much to say. I think maybe Grandma told Mom about it, but it wasn't something that Mom and I ever discussed."

"I wish you hadn't been alone with that," Shannon said, and I sighed.

"I've never been all that good at spilling my guts," I said. "I just wanted to...I don't know. Not forget it, but put it away maybe?"

"And now Cade's back, and you're back..."

"He seems so angry still," I mused. "I know he was pretty angry after he left, but shouldn't he have gotten over that? It was so long ago."

"Who knows?" Shannon shrugged. "Just because he's back doesn't mean that you have to do anything about it. If he doesn't care for you, you don't have to care for him. You can leave each other be."

She rose to take my empty bowl of stew, setting my reward of pie in front of me. We talked about other things: the endless discussion about what to do about the house, how Chloe was doing, and throughout all of it, I couldn't stop my mind from sneaking back to Cade.

I don't know if Shannon knew that leaving Cade alone was easier said than done. From the moment we met, we had never been able to leave each other alone if the other was near; not until he rode away from me that spring night almost a decade ago.

Now that we were both in White Pines again, who knew what would happen.

If you want to continue reading this story, you can get your copy from your favorite vendor by searching for the title:

Destined Desires

A Bad Boy Billionaire Romance

You can also find the e-book version by typing this link in your computer's browser:

https://www.hotandsteamyromance.com/products/destined-desires-a-second-chance-romance

OTHER BOOKS BY THIS AUTHOR

Saving Her Rescuer: A Billionaire & A Virgin Romance

I was just trying to get away from my crazy ex for the weekend when I ended up in a giant pileup on the highway up to Gore Mountain.

https://geni.us/SavingHerRescuer

Sensual Sounds: A Rockstar Ménage

Lust. Lies. Double lives.

The rock and roll industry is full of people who are looking out for themselves and willing to do anything to rise to the top.

https://www.hotandsteamyromance.com/collections/frontpage/products/sensual-sounds-a-rockstar-menage

---

On the Run: A Secret Baby Romance

Murder. Lies. Fraud. Just another day in the lives of billionaires and women on the run.

https://www.hotandsteamyromance.com/collections/frontpage/products/on-the-run-a-secret-baby-romance

The Dirty Doctor's Touch: A Billionaire Doctor Romance

I am a master. An elitist. I am at the top of my field, and I know what I am doing.

https://www.hotandsteamyromance.com/collections/frontpage/products/the-dirty-doctor-s-touch-a-billionaire-doctor-romance

∾

The Hero She Needs: A Single Daddy Next Door Romance

He's the only man I've ever wanted...

https://www.hotandsteamyromance.com/collections/frontpage/products/the-hero-she-needs-a-single-daddy-next-door-romance

∾

You can find all of my books here:

Hot and Steamy Romance

https://www.hotandsteamyromance.com

∾

Facebook

facebook.com/HotAndSteamyRomance

COPYRIGHT

©Copyright 2020 by Alizeh Valentine - All rights Reserved
In no way is it legal to reproduce, duplicate, or transmit any part of this document in either electronic means or in printed format. Recording of this publication is strictly prohibited and any storage of this document is not allowed unless with written permission from the publisher. All rights are reserved. Respective authors own all copyrights not held by the publisher.

www.ingramcontent.com/pod-product-compliance
Lightning Source LLC
LaVergne TN
LVHW011728060526
838200LV00051B/3068